D0090420

KRAZYLAND

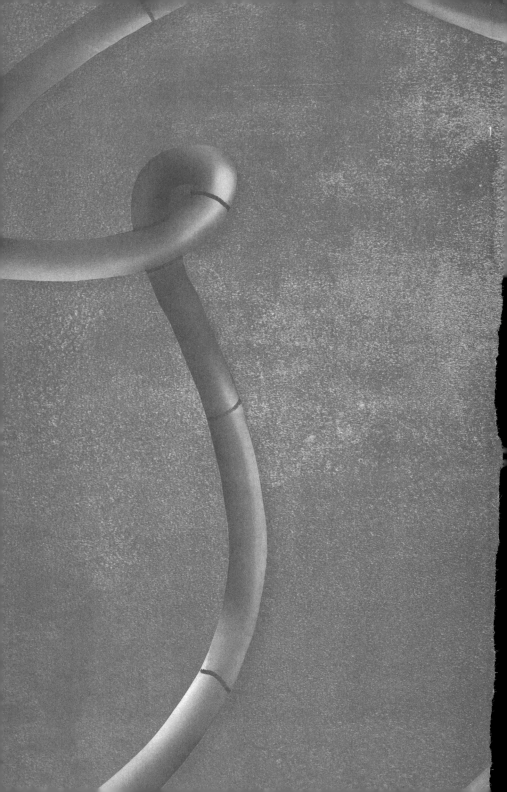

KRAZYLAND

MAR ROMASCO-MOORE

DELACORTE PRESS

Text copyright © 2022 by Maria Romasco Moore
Jacket art copyright © 2022 by Alexander Jansson

All rights reserved. Published in the United States by Delacorte Press, an imprint of Random House Children's Books, a division of Penguin Random House LLC, New York.

Delacorte Press is a registered trademark and the colophon is a trademark of Penguin Random House LLC.

Visit us on the Web! rhcbooks.com

Educators and librarians, for a variety of teaching tools, visit us at RHTeachersLibrarians.com

Library of Congress Cataloging-in-Publication Data is available upon request.
ISBN 978-0-593-48687-0 (trade pbk.) — ISBN 978-0-593-48688-7 (ebook)

The text of this book is set in 12-point Archer.
Interior design by Heather Kelly

Printed in the United States of America
10 9 8 7 6 5 4 3 2 1
First Edition

UNHAPPY BIRTHDAY

There was icing in my nose. Icing in my eyes. Vanilla buttercream, with blue and purple roses. Though the roses were all smashed beyond recognition now.

I couldn't see, but I could hear the cackling of my older cousin Jake, the one who had just shoved me face-first into a cake, and the indignant shrieks of my younger cousin Jenny, whose name had been written on said cake. I would happily have given up all cake for the rest of my life in exchange for instant transportation to anywhere else in the world.

I hadn't even wanted to come to this birthday party. Nothing against Jenny personally, but she was four years younger than me, and so were most of her friends. I was thirteen, much too old to hang out with fourth graders.

I pushed myself up and wiped the icing from my eyes. Jake was smirking at me. He was three years older than me and at least a foot and a half taller, and he never let me forget either of those facts.

"Now, what's all this?" My uncle Steven appeared at the door to the party room with a stack of paper plates. Jenny ran over to him, wailing, and tugged on his beige STAFF T-shirt.

"Nathan fell in the cake," said Jake.

Uncle Steven gave him a skeptical look, but there was little hope he would take my side. Jake was his son, after all.

"Go cover the front desk for a while" was all he said, waving a hand.

My uncle owned this place, and Jake was working here over the summer. No doubt I'd have to work here someday, too. Uncle Steven bought it two years ago, and since then practically every family event has been held in the neon-painted party room.

My uncle could at least have owned a normal business. Maybe an ice-cream shop or a movie theater, so I would benefit from unlimited soft serve or free matinees.

Instead, he owned Krazyland.

STEALTHY VEGETABLES

Krazyland Kids Indoor Playplace was, according to a sign in the lobby, "the perfect space for kids to get the exercise they need while having the fun they crave," which made it sound like one of those fruit juices that have pictures of strawberries on the front but are actually like 75 percent pureed carrots.

It was a converted warehouse. Half the building was filled with mechanical games that spat out tickets you could swap for cheap plastic prizes. The other half was filled with a maze of giant plastic tubes that looped around and around like the multicolored guts of a giant.

I'd been there a few times before my uncle bought it—for instance, in second grade, when this guy Kyle invited the entire class to his birthday party. I remember he looked vaguely disappointed when I showed up. No doubt it had been his parents' idea to include everybody, even the kids Kyle didn't particularly like.

Kids like me.

The owner back then had been an old guy with a gray beard and weird glasses. I could remember turning in my tickets to him at the prize counter once.

"I see great promise in you, young man," he said as he handed over my beanbag frog. "Do not be discouraged if the world does not fit you."

I blinked at him, too confused to respond, and then scurried off to hide in a corner until Kyle's birthday party was over.

When Uncle Steven did buy the place—I think that old guy had died or something—my parents assumed I'd be delighted. I could get in free now, after all. They thought I'd want to go every day.

True, I enjoyed some of the arcade games, though many of them had bad graphics or fiddly controls. A lot of them—like the claw machines, which held the same junk as the bottom shelf of the prize counter—were also just blatant cash grabs.

The Skee-Ball lanes and the spider-stomping game were all right. And the tubes and trampolines had been fun when I was younger.

But at the end of the day, Krazyland was just too loud, too crowded. Too full of the bane of my existence: other kids. I was much happier at home, where it was safe and quiet. If it was up to me, I'd spend all my time in my room, alone, playing *Voidjumper*.

ESCAPE

T he morning of Jenny's party had been perfect. It was summer. No school. No responsibilities.

I rolled out of bed and went directly to my computer.

Fifteen minutes later, I was running for my life, pursued by ten flying eyeballs.

I didn't dare stop to look at them, but I knew they were there. Big white blobs the size of my head, trailing optic nerves like tails. Bright green laser beams shot from their pupils, barely missing me as I dodged and swerved.

I skidded around the corner and down the next hallway.

This world was all one big house. Endless, without windows. Plenty of doors, though.

I opened one at random. Beyond it was yet another hallway, with hideous procedurally generated wallpaper. I sprinted until my energy failed.

The next door I flung open led to a kitchen. I opened every cabinet, searching for a way out of the world.

The green light of the eyeball lasers pierced through the doorway.

I tried the refrigerator. A takeout container on the top shelf yielded a mysterious specimen, which I popped into my inventory to investigate later.

The first eyeball burst into the room. I yanked the lid from a pot on the stove and held it up as a shield. Just in time. The lasers deflected harmlessly.

I was just about to run again when I spotted it. There, revealed when I'd pulled off the lid: inky blackness, a hint of stars. The void, floating in a soup tureen.

The other nine eyeballs had crowded into the kitchen now, their lasers lighting the room up like a disco. I climbed atop the stove, thankful that I still had a shrinking potion in my inventory. I drank it, jumping at the same time. A laser swept the space where my head had been an instant before. I fell into the pot.

And kept on falling right out of the world, into the void.

"Nathan!"

My mother's voice startled me so much I dropped the controller. I fumbled for it and hit pause.

"You haven't even had breakfast yet," Mom said from where she stood in the doorway, disapproval radiating off her in waves.

"It's summer break," I said.

She sighed. Last summer, I'd spent almost every day playing *Voidjumper*. I'd visited hundreds of worlds, solving puzzles and collecting items to bring back to my base world, which I'd built into a perfect digital paradise, just for me.

"You need to get ready," she said. "We're leaving in an hour."

I'd forgotten all about the party.

"Aw, come on," I said. "Do I really have to go? Jenny probably doesn't even want me there."

"Family is important, Nathan."

"Okay, sure," I said, frantically trying to come up with an argument that would appeal to Mom. I was good with words—it was my main line of defense. "But remember that time I sprained my ankle on the trampolines? Krazyland is just too dangerous. Surely, you would not be so heartless as to expose your one and only precious baby boy to certain grievous bodily harm?"

Mom merely raised an eyebrow. I was losing.

"I'm just saying it would be far safer for me to stay home," I grumbled.

"Seventy-five percent of accidents requiring hospital visits occur in the home," said my mother flatly. "It would be safer for you not to."

LOST . . .

Which was how I'd ended up here, in the Krazyland bathroom, scraping cake crumbs out of my hair. I tried to reassure myself that it could be worse. At least I was better off than my best friend, Rudy, whose parents shipped him off to camp every summer. He'd texted me yesterday:

help bugs everywhere

no signal except in 1 spot

everybody fights 4 it

I may not survive

As far as I could tell, camp was like school but worse. Most of the "fun" activities sounded suspiciously like gym class. At least with school you get to leave every afternoon. At camp you're stuck, surrounded by other kids twenty-four seven. No escape.

If only there were a void in every pot.

I eyed the bathroom door. What if when I opened it, it didn't lead to Krazyland? I closed my eyes, concentrated every ounce of my will on wishing hard, and flung the door open.

I was greeted by the piercing screams of small children and the wafting scent of greasy pizza.

Still here.

The door trick never worked, of course, no matter how many times I tried it. And I'd tried it a lot, with many different doors.

Alas, the door to the boys' locker room at school only ever led directly to gym class. At least the trick of pretending to have a stomachache so I could go to the nurse's office worked some of the time.

I tracked down Uncle Steven in the small kitchen. Krazyland offered pizza by the slice and fried chicken wings by the bucket. Uncle Steven himself prepared these items. I say *prepare* instead of *cook* because all he did was dump them out of the box they came in directly into the deep fryer or the microwave.

"Hello, esteemed ancestor," I said, sidling up to my uncle. "Terribly sorry to bother you, but I seem to be suffering a modicum of digestive distress."

"Uh-huh," he said, without turning. I'd expected more

of a response than that. I'd even busted out several advanced vocabulary words. Adults usually ate up that kind of thing.

"I think perhaps I'd better go home right away to *convalesce*."

He shot me a harried look. "What are you talking about?"

Before I could try again, a woman appeared at the ordering window with a sour expression.

"Excuse me," she said to Uncle Steven, and then again, louder, without waiting for him to respond. "EXCUSE ME."

"Yes?"

"I can't find my kid."

He pointed to a small sign posted just below the menu beside the ordering window, one of many such signs posted all over the building.

IT IS NOT OUR RESPONSIBILITY TO WATCH THE CHILDREN said the sign.

"Yes, fine," said the woman, "but we've got taekwondo in fifteen and I can't find Brayden anywhere."

Uncle Steven pulled a walkie-talkie from his belt, pressed a button. His announcement crackled over the loudspeaker: "Would Brayden please report to the kitchen area."

He went back to work disaffectedly jiggling the deep-fryer basket. The woman remained at the window, shifting impatiently from foot to foot, scanning the playroom beyond, checking her watch, clearing her throat. Uncle Steven sighed.

His eye turned, regrettably, to me.

"Nathan," he said as my heart sank, "how'd you like to be a big help?"

... AND FOUND

'm too old for this, I thought, as five-, six-, seven-, and eight-year-olds went careening past me, high on sugar, practically levitating with hyper glee.

In truth, the twisting tubes had once been my favorite part of Krazyland. I liked the way you could get totally lost in their mazes.

But even though I was still short for my age, they felt so much smaller and more cramped than they had just a few years earlier. The hard, curved plastic was murder on the knees, and I'd already been kicked twice. I was also faintly worried someone from my school might see me crawling around in here and deem me even more uncool than I was already.

The blue tunnel I was crawling through slanted suddenly downward. I slid, landed in the second-biggest ball pit. There were three kids in there already, all of them slinging balls at each other's heads. As soon as I got to my feet I was struck in the ear with a deafening *thwack* of hollow plastic.

"Are any of you named Brayden?" I shouted amid a hail of plastic projectiles.

When there was no answer, I picked up a ball and whaled it at the nearest kid's head. He ducked, vanishing below the surface before popping up again a few feet away and throwing another ball at me.

The lady had given me a description of her missing kid: age six, blond hair, striped shirt, blue shorts, "adorable." None of these kids matched, so I waded laboriously out of the pit, pelted from all sides.

After that, I circled around to the smallest ball pit. It appeared empty.

"Brayden," I shouted just in case, "your mom left. She said to tell you she doesn't want you anymore and you can just live here from now on."

When several moments passed with neither a cry of dismay nor a whoop of joy, I moved on to the largest ball pit. It was way in the back of the building, near the entrance to the stockroom, and about the size of a small swimming pool.

"Hey, everybody," I shouted, "there's free pizza for the first ten people who show up to the dining area. Better hurry!"

My lie emptied the ball pit in no time. I scanned each kid who scrambled down the foam steps. No striped shirt.

I was about to turn away when a sound made me pause. I stared hard at the surface of the ball pit.

And there it was. Ever so slight, a shifting. Just the barest hint of movement over at the far end of the pit, a few balls settling.

I climbed the foam steps and waded in. Walking through plastic balls is surprisingly hard. Halfway across I hit a weird spot. There must have been a hole in the mesh at the bottom of the pit or something because I took a step and felt my foot sinking. I flailed, unbalanced.

"Arrgh!" I cried, gripped with a brief panic. My foot was stuck, somehow.

On the other side of the pit, a kid with blond hair and a striped shirt emerged in a sudden explosion of balls. He made a run for the nearest tube. With one enormous burst of effort, I wrenched my foot free of whatever was holding it and lunged at the escaping figure, managing to snag the back of his shirt with one hand.

"Brayden?" I asked.

"No," he said, "I'm a shark."

"Your mother is looking for you. Come on." I dragged him toward the foam stairs.

"No!" he cried, wriggling mightily. "I hate taekwondo. They kick you."

"Who does?"

"The other kids."

"Well, kick them back. Isn't that the point?"

"I'm scared," he wailed.

"If we didn't do the things we're scared of," I said, "we'd never do anything at all."

I felt silly as soon as the words left my lips. It was something my mother said to me. I'd always thought it was dumb, so why was I repeating it?

Anyway, I'd probably have hated taekwondo, too. Anything that even remotely resembled gym class was my idea of a rotten time. The problem isn't that I'm bad at sports and running and stuff like that. I'm not. The problem is that everybody takes one look at me—a chubby kid—and assumes I am. The only kind of exercise I like is the kind you do alone, with nobody there to make fun of you.

I was about to say something to Brayden about how I felt his pain, when I was interrupted by a low rumbling, like distant thunder. The sound seemed to come, improbably, from below us. We both froze.

"Did you hear that?" I asked.

Brayden nodded, eyes wide. In the silence that followed, the noise came again. Except this time, it didn't sound like thunder.

This time, I could have sworn it sounded like a voice.

I waited a moment, but I didn't hear anything else. The longer I stood there, the less sure I was that I'd even heard anything to begin with.

But Brayden had stopped squirming. When I herded him once more toward the exit, he didn't resist.

...AND LOST AGAIN

After I'd delivered Brayden to his mother, I reached for my phone to see how much longer I had until the party was over. Maybe I'd text Rudy, too. No doubt he was being forced to learn canoeing or underwater basket weaving, so at least we could commiserate.

But my phone was gone.

I made a frantic circuit of the building, eyes on the floor, checking every dark corner. There was plenty of trash and lost tickets strewn about, but no phone. Resigned, I crawled back through the endless plastic tunnels, trying to retrace the route I'd taken in my search for Brayden.

My search hit a wall at the first ball pit. A wall of balls. If the phone had slipped out of my pocket while I was in there, it would have fallen to the bottom, but it was impossible to see down there. I kept trying to push the balls out of the way, but others would just flood in to take their place, no matter how fast I dug.

"Having fun in there?" asked Jake. My head snapped up. He was grinning at me through the mesh sides of the pit.

"I lost my phone," I said.

"Oh yeah? What brand was it, Fisher-Price?"

"No, it was regular. With a *Voidjumper* case. Have you seen it?"

"*Voidjumper*? That game is for babies."

I sighed. I shouldn't have bothered. "It isn't. Adults play it."

"Yeah, adults who are babies."

"That's a contradiction," I told him. I might have been shorter and younger and weaker than him, but at least I was smarter.

"Your face is a contradiction," he shot back.

Seething, I returned to the kitchen to tell Uncle Steven about my missing phone.

"Go ahead and put a note on the lost and found," he told me, gesturing to a bulletin board on the far wall. It was overflowing with so many notes you could barely see the board itself.

"Will that help?" I asked.

Uncle Steven shrugged. "John the security guard used to oversee lost items, but he skipped town a few months back and I haven't found a replacement. I'm sure we'll all keep an eye out, though."

Great, so they'd even lost the guy in charge of the lost and found.

"I think it might have fallen into the ball pits," I said. "Do you ever empty them out?"

Uncle Steven blinked at me as though he didn't understand. "Empty?"

"You know," I prompted, "like for cleaning."

"Ah," he said slowly. Too slowly. "Yes. The ball pits. Cleaning. Of course. That is definitely a thing we do."

He didn't quite meet my eyes.

"Well are you going to do it anytime soon?" I pressed. "Empty the pits?"

"I . . . Oh, goodness, will you look at that." Uncle Steven made a show of noticing something in the middle distance and hurried off.

EVERYTHING

I stopped by the prize counter, which was unattended, and helped myself to a novelty watch that had animals instead of numbers. Technically I hadn't earned enough tickets, but I planned to return it as soon as I found my phone. The watch informed me that I still had two hours of compulsory fun to suffer through.

Jenny and her friends had been released from the party room. They swept across Krazyland now like a sugar-fueled conquering horde.

I passed a group of them crowded around the spider-stomping game. It was meant for one person to play at a time—you stood on a platform with eight plastic pedals in the shape of spiders. The pedals lit up one by one at random. As soon as a pedal lit up, you had to stomp on it.

The birthday group were all stomping on the pedals at once. As I watched, the machine gave a terrible shudder, let out a little puff of black smoke, and then sat there beeping mournfully.

Undaunted, Jenny and her friends moved on to the next game over: Big Bertha.

Big Bertha was one of the weirder games at Krazyland, which is saying something. She was essentially just a big cloth bag with some yarn hair and black plastic eyes that looked in two different directions. Her mouth took up half her face. To win the game, you threw colored plastic balls, the same ones that filled Krazyland's three ball pits, into her mouth. Points for each successful throw were labeled as weight gained.

As a chubby guy myself, I always felt uncomfortable playing the Bertha game. My mom said when I hit my growth spurt I'd "stretch right out," which honestly sounded like something from a horror movie. Really, I just wished everyone would leave me alone about it. The Bertha game seemed designed to make fun of people like me. Jake and the kids at school already did enough of that. They didn't need any help.

I decided my best bet now was to go hide in the empty party room.

When I got there, though, I discovered it wasn't empty after all. There was a girl slumped over in the corner with her head resting on a large inflatable bear from the prize counter, apparently asleep.

I didn't recognize her, but she wore a khaki staff shirt

with the Krazyland logo (a capital letter *K* with googly eyes) stitched poorly above the breast pocket. She looked maybe about Jake's age. Must be one of the summer hires. Surely, she wouldn't want to be caught sleeping on the job.

"Uh, hello?" I tried. "HELLO."

When she didn't stir, I prodded her very gently in the side with the toe of my sneaker before retreating a few feet. Her eyes snapped open at once.

"Who are you?" she demanded, glaring at me.

"I'm Nathan, Steven's nephew."

"Mercy," she said.

"What?"

"That's my name." She rolled her eyes, got to her feet, and started gathering paper cake plates to clear away.

"I'm sure you could have some if you wanted," I said, gesturing at the leftover cake sitting at one end of the table. There were still a few un-smashed slices left. "My uncle wouldn't mind."

"I'm allergic," Mercy said.

"To cake?"

"To everything," she said, before sweeping out of the party room.

WHERE IT
GETS BAD

The empty party room was peaceful, but a little boring. I had no phone to distract me. No friends to talk to.

Not that I usually had friends to talk to anyway. The truth is that Rudy was my only real friend. I'd sent him an email the night before, but I knew they were only allowed to use the camp computers once a day.

The thing was: even when Rudy wasn't away at summer camp, he still lived four states away from me.

Rudy and I had never actually met face to face. We'd met online and chatted via Discord or text, mostly. My mom talked to his mom on the phone once, to make sure neither of us were secretly fifty-year-old men (we weren't).

Rudy loved *Voidjumper* as much as I did. Maybe more, honestly. He was a weird kid just like me. We understood each other. Nobody I knew in real life was like that.

I closed my eyes, tried to tune out the muffled shouting of children in the distance and the occasional loudspeaker announcements reminding everyone that *shoes are not to be worn in the play tunnels* or demanding that some kid or another *report immediately to the front desk.*

The strange moment from the large ball pit came back to me, the noise I'd heard. Maybe it had just been a weird echo.

Sometime after fox-thirty (which my prize-counter watch marked by emitting a digitized yipping) I became aware that multiple voices in the distance were shouting the same thing. A name: Ronald.

I peered out the party room door and saw several adults rushing around, seemingly looking for a kid. Cautiously, I emerged and spotted Uncle Steven near the front entrance, talking to a man and a woman in blue uniforms. My stomach twisted. The police.

"Oh, too bad," said Jake from behind me. "You're still here. I thought you'd disappeared, too."

"What?" I spun around. "Why are the police here?"

"They're probably here to arrest you for being criminally uncool."

"Stop it." I genuinely felt a little nauseous now. "Tell me for real."

Jake shrugged. "One of Jenny's annoying little friends is missing. His parents came to pick him up, but nobody can find him."

"He's probably just hiding in the ball pit," I said, thinking of Brayden.

"I checked there," said Jake.

I thought about asking him if he'd heard any mysterious, otherworldly voices, but no doubt he'd just mock me.

Uncle Steven approached us a moment later looking grim.

"There's no sign of this Ronald kid and the parents are freaking out." He nodded toward a tearful couple who were now speaking to the two police officers. "We'll all need to give statements."

"But he's probably just hiding or something, right?" I insisted.

Uncle Steven shrugged. "Hopefully he'll turn up, but we really have looked all over. We've even checked the security tapes." He frowned. "Usually, I have the opposite problem. We go to close up for the night and find some kid wandering around whose parents just dropped them off and left. You'd think I was running a daycare!"

The two cops came over. One of them went with Uncle Steven to the back office to review the footage from Krazyland's many security cameras. The other, to my horror, wanted to speak to the kids who had been attending the party, which included me.

"Seen or heard anything suspicious today?" she asked, after my identity as Steven's nephew had been established.

"Um." I thought again of the strange rumbling noise from the ball pit earlier. "Maybe." But I couldn't tell her about that. She'd think I was making things up. "No."

"Maybe no?"

My watch chose that moment to emit a loud digital quack. My hand flew to my pocket.

"What was that?" the cop asked.

"Sorry, ma'am," I said. "It's duck o'clock."

She narrowed her eyes at me. "This is a very serious matter, kid. Now answer me straight, have you witnessed anything unusual lately?"

I did not appreciate being called "kid." The snot-nosed knee-highs running around screaming were kids. I was a jaded and world-weary thirteen. Thir-*teen*. Not thir-child.

"No," I said firmly.

WHERE IT GETS STRANGE

When Ronald still failed to appear, the police decided they had to treat it as a possible kidnapping. They issued a county-wide alert and Krazyland shut down for the day.

All the other kids and parents filtered out until the only people left were me, my relatives, and Mercy. There was a moment when it seemed like Mercy was missing, too, but it turned out she was just back in the stockroom, asleep atop a pile of cardboard boxes.

"I know the police did their search," said my uncle after we'd all been rounded up, "but I want to do one more sweep of the place before I leave. And don't worry," he said to Jake and Mercy, "I'll still pay you two for your full hours even though we're closing early." He turned to me then. "Nathan, you can wait up front here with Jenny or I can call your parents to come get you if you're scared."

Jake snorted. My heart sank.

Going home was all I had wanted an hour before, but I knew how bad it would look if I admitted to being scared in front of Jake. And Mercy.

"No," I said, "I'll help."

"Okay," said Uncle Steven. "Thanks. You stick with your cousin."

I trudged after Jake as he headed toward the back of the building. It was eerily quiet without any kids in the place.

"What's the deal with Mercy?" I asked him once we'd gotten out of earshot of the others.

"Why? You got a crush on her or something? Because bad news, she likes girls. Not that anyone would ever go for a little nerd like you anyway."

"No! I just hadn't seen her around before. Seems like she sleeps a lot."

Jake made a noise of disgust. "Ugh, yeah. You'd think I would be the one who could get away with slacking off, but no, apparently she's the one who can do whatever she wants." He knelt to peer under the trampolines.

"Isn't she worried about getting fired?"

"Nah. I think Dad mostly hired her out of pity. Her grandfather is the one who started this place, and I guess her family was having a hard time or whatever after he died. Can you fit under there?"

This last was in reference to the narrow space beneath the trampolines. It was dark and dusty. But I had offered to help, hadn't I?

I lowered myself to my stomach and army-crawled in. The light filtering through the weave of the trampolines cast strange patterns on the floor. There didn't seem to be any place a child could hide, though.

And then I heard a telltale creak of springs. Jake was climbing onto the trampolines! He was going to jump and crush me! Frantically I squirmed back out from beneath them.

Jake laughed when he saw my panic-stricken expression. "Wow," he said. "Chill out, man. Don't be such a wimp."

He strode off toward the Skee-Ball lanes. I decided I'd had enough of sticking with him and headed instead toward the big ball pit. Maybe I should see if I could hear anything else weird.

Mercy, however, had beaten me there. She was standing next to the entrance of the pit, staring in.

"Hey," I said.

She turned, gave me a curious look. "If you thought you knew where the missing kid went," she said, "what would you do?"

"Um, tell the police?"

She shook her head. "They wouldn't believe me."

Unease gnawed at me. The voice. Had she heard it, too? Should I ask her about it?

"*Do* you know where he is?" I asked instead.

Mercy sighed. "I might."

She kicked off her sneakers and stepped to the top of the foam stairs in one stride.

"You probably shouldn't follow me," she said, and then she jumped.

It was a hell of a jump. A proper cannonball. As if she were jumping into a real pool, not a shallow, rainbow cesspit of germs and polypropylene.

There was a *whumpf,* an explosion of bright plastic balls, and then stillness.

"Mercy?" I said, when she did not emerge after a moment.

Nothing. No movement. No sound. I watched the surface of the pit, but I didn't spot even the slightest shifting.

I pulled my own shoes off and ran up the foam steps.

"Mercy!" I shouted down at the pit. "What are you doing?"

You can't drown in a ball pit, right? Maybe if you really worked at it . . .

"Mercy!" I yelled again. There was no answer. So, I did the only thing I could think of: I jumped.

I jumped—and this where it gets strange—I jumped and I fell.

You might think that this is not so strange a thing at all. Gravity does tend to have that effect. But this pit had been designed for children. The depth of those plastic balls was three and a half feet at most. I'm short but not that short. My feet should have hit the mesh and foam floor of the pit right away.

Yet they did not. I fell.

Falling through densely packed hollow plastic balls is a strange sensation, not unlike being gently punched all over by a thousand fists.

It was starting to feel as if I might just go on like this forever, when suddenly I became aware that, although still falling, I was no longer surrounded by plastic balls.

I was now falling through open air.

It was at this point, and not until this point, that I screamed.

NOTHING

I landed and bounced, the ground stretching beneath me in a way that ground absolutely has no right to before catapulting me back into the air. I landed again, bounced again.

Finally, I landed for good, sprawled flat on my back. The ground rippled beneath me and then was still.

I was not dead.

This might seem obvious now, but it was not at the time. I allowed myself to check, reaching my hands unsteadily to my face. It was still there. My fingers were there. I wiggled my toes. Yup, still there. I carried out a brief but thorough inventory of my other vital components—which I will refrain from listing in full for the sake of decency—and was relieved to find them all present and accounted for.

Well, that was something, anyway.

I was looking up at an enormous gray cloud. It filled the sky from horizon to horizon, as far as I could see in any direction. As I stared at the cloud, I realized that it was not gray at all, but multicolored, made of tiny specks of red and blue and yellow and green. Like television static or colored newsprint.

I rolled over and pushed myself to my feet, causing a slight undulation of the ground. I say ground, but it was of course not ground at all.

I was standing on an enormous trampoline. From where I stood, I could see no edge to it. It just stretched on and on, the same way as the cloud. In the space between these two expanses, cloud above and trampoline below, there was nothing.

And I really do mean nothing. There wasn't even sky. It was not like the void of *Voidjumper,* black pierced with white pixel stars. The horizon here wasn't black or white or gray. It wasn't any color at all.

It hurt my eyes to look at it. They seemed to be registering the ocular nerve version of an error code. There was nothing to focus on.

I started to shake. Just slightly, shivering as if cold. But I wasn't cold.

This was what I'd always dreamed of. I'd found a way out of the normal world and into some other place. I should have been thrilled, ecstatic.

Instead, I was terrified. It had been so sudden—the rug of the entire universe being pulled out from under me.

The shaking, at least, was something I'd experienced before. The first time it happened to me, my mother had helped me understand. This was a panic attack—when fear gets so strong it takes over your whole body.

I dropped back to my knees on the trampoline, tried my best to breathe slowly in and out the way my mother had shown me—though my brain insisted that breathing super-fast and shallow was the way to go.

"I did tell you not to follow me" came a voice from behind me.

I spun around to find Mercy, regarding me coolly with a hand on her hip.

"What's going on?" I gasped. "Where are we?"

"Nowhere," she said.

"What?"

"Nowhere," she repeated.

If she was as freaked out as I was, she certainly wasn't showing it. In fact, she looked quite at ease. She was even smiling.

"How are you so calm?" I demanded, unable to keep a note of hysteria out of my voice.

Mercy glanced down at my shaking hands. "It's okay," she said. "Don't worry. I've been here before."

"You've been here before?"

"Well, not *here* exactly, but another place like this."

Her eyes shifted to something behind me and her

expression changed. She didn't look scared exactly, but suddenly she didn't look so calm, either.

She began to slowly back away.

"You probably don't want to turn around right now," she said.

TURNABOUT
IS FAIR PLAY

I turned, an act I regretted immediately as it brought me face to face (or more accurately, face to chelicerae) with the most enormous spider I had ever seen.

The thing towered over me, eight hairy legs like telephone poles and a swollen black body the size of my mother's car. Each of its eight glistening eyes was the size of my head and each of them, as far as I could tell, was staring straight at me.

So, you know that right there was more than bad enough. Nightmare fuel for at least a month or two.

But that wasn't even the weird part.

The weird part was that at the end of each of the spider's eight enormous legs was a small black shoe. Eight little high tops with red laces. I might have thought it was funny if I weren't so busy being terrified.

I turned back around and ran. Mercy was already off, running far ahead of me.

Everybody always picks me last in gym, but I'm actually a really fast runner when I need to be. My dad had tried to get me to join track, but there was no way I was going to voluntarily wear gym shorts in public.

Unfortunately, it is almost impossible to run well when the ground is a trampoline. I bounced with every step and had to work just to keep my balance.

Up ahead, I saw that the never-ending trampoline did end after all. It stopped short maybe fifty feet away from me. Beyond: that sickening nothingness. Mercy was almost to the edge already.

I couldn't help it. Still running, I looked over my shoulder. Eight massive eyes looked back. The thing was practically right on top of me.

I stumbled and tripped.

Scrabbling on the slick fabric of the trampoline, I managed to roll so I was faceup. I'm not sure that was any better, because now I could see the spider as it towered over me. Some unknown liquid dripped from its complex arachnid mouthparts. I thought I saw a flash of fangs.

I tried to scramble to my feet, but before I could, the spider lifted one of its telephone-pole legs high in the air and slammed it down right in the middle of my chest.

The blow knocked the breath out of me. My vision went white. I squirmed and gasped for air.

When I could finally see straight, my eyes focused on the toe of the black sneaker pinning me to the ground.

I tried to shout for Mercy to help me, but all that came out was a strangled whine. I turned my head just in time to see her run right off the edge of the trampoline. One second she was there and the next second—gone.

I strained against the weight of the spider's leg, but that only made it press down more. It was hard to get a full breath. My vision was blurring at the edges. My lungs burned. Finally, in desperation, I went limp.

Okay, I thought. *I give up.* For a moment I felt as if I was viewing myself from a distance. I'd experienced this once or twice, too: dissociation, when fear gets so strong that your brain tries to run away from your body.

"Nathan!"

The distant sound of Mercy's voice startled me back into myself. Honestly, I think I was just surprised she'd remembered my name.

With a burst of panic-fueled strength, I rolled hard to the left. It was just enough. I popped free, scrambled to my feet, and sprinted like hell to the end of the trampoline.

About ten or fifteen feet down, slightly offset, there was another enormous floating trampoline. Mercy stood there with her hands on her hips, looking up expectantly.

I glanced behind me. The spider was loping toward me, gaining quickly.

I jumped, bounced, landed in a crouch a few feet from Mercy.

"What the hell was that," I gasped.

"A spider," said Mercy.

I was going to tell her to stop treating me like an idiot but the trampoline above us was shaking. A black high-top sneaker with red laces appeared at the edge of it, followed quickly by seven more.

I shrieked and started running again, Mercy close behind me. At the end of this trampoline was another. And beyond that was yet another, and beyond that . . . well, you get the idea.

"I think we lost it," said Mercy, after we'd jumped across maybe a dozen giant trampolines.

My legs ached. Exhausted, terrified, I curled up into a small ball and shut my eyes, hoping that when I opened them none of this would be happening. I was shivering again, teeth chattering, all the built-up terror shaking me apart.

"Nathan?" I heard Mercy say. She touched my shoulder lightly and then pulled her hand away. "It wasn't real, you know."

"What?" I opened my eyes.

"Just, if it makes you feel any better, that spider wasn't real."

"You were running, too," I pointed out.

"Well, yeah," she said. "Just because something isn't real, doesn't mean it can't hurt you."

An involuntary cry of anguish escaped my lips and I squeezed my eyes shut again.

"Nathan," Mercy said, "chill out, it's fine now."

"You don't know what it was like," I said. "I thought it was going to crush me. It was standing on my chest with its horrible massive leg and I couldn't breathe."

Mercy laughed. A big throaty laugh.

I bristled, eyes snapping open. "It wasn't funny."

"It was trying to stomp you!" Mercy exclaimed, between bouts of laughter.

"What are you talking about?" I sat up, annoyance momentarily crowding out my fear. And then, suddenly, I got it.

In Krazyland, there was a game where you stomped spiders. Here, wherever the hell *here* was, spiders apparently stomped you.

I guess it was only fair.

Mercy's laughter petered out. She settled on the trampoline cross-legged and gazed out into the nothingness, seemingly content.

"I still don't understand," I said. "This is nowhere? And it's real but not real? And you've been here but you haven't been here."

Mercy shrugged. "It's complicated."

"Well, can you explain?"

"You wouldn't understand."

"I might."

"You wouldn't."

This was all hard enough to take in without Mercy treating me like I was dumber than a rock. I was, in fact, a great deal smarter than a rock.

"Stop treating me like an idiot," I said.

Mercy looked genuinely startled. It was hard to tell, since her face was so sunburnt already, but I was pretty sure her cheeks went a little red. "Oh," she said. "Sorry. I'm not very good with people."

"Yeah, that's obvious." I was still feeling annoyed, which was good, because it distracted me from being scared.

I glanced at the horizon, but my eyes slid off the horrible nothingness like grease. Everything about this place felt wrong. Too empty. Too still. Too quiet.

No sooner had I thought this than I heard the voice.

I thought it was thunder at first and instinctively looked up to the mottled cloud overhead, half expecting rain.

But it couldn't have been thunder. Thunder doesn't speak English.

NOWHERE IS A PLACE

"**M**ORE," the voice had said, in a tone like tectonic plates shifting deep beneath the surface of the earth.

"What was that?" I asked Mercy.

"I have no idea," she said, which was almost a relief. At least I wasn't the only one in the dark for once.

The thunderous voice boomed out again in the distance. It was impossible to tell which direction it was coming from. Perhaps it was coming from everywhere at once.

"Will you at least *try* to tell me what you do know about this place?" I said, when the echoes died away. "Please?"

"Okay," said Mercy. She sounded reluctant. "But you can't tell anyone else. You have to promise."

Who would I tell? I thought about mentioning to her that I only had one friend in the world and he was stuck at summer camp hundreds of miles (and possibly a whole dimension) away, but settled for: "I promise."

"Well," she said, "emanationist metaphysics proposes the existence of a physical plane, encompassing visible reality, with this physical universe being only one of several nested planes of existence."

"Wait, what?"

Mercy smirked. "I knew you wouldn't understand."

"Now hold on, you were being overcomplicated on purpose. Not fair."

She sighed. "Fine. Everything has an opposite. And the real world is *somewhere* and everything in it is *something*. No matter where you go in the world, even the most remote corner of it, you are still somewhere. Does that make sense?"

I nodded.

"Now imagine the opposite of that. A place that is genuinely *nowhere*, full of *nothing*. And not the way that Iowa is full of nothing. Corn still counts. But really nothing."

She pointed to the horizon. To the greasy, colorless slick of space where my eyes could find no purchase.

"Like that," she said.

"Okay," I said. If that stuff (or rather not-stuff) out there was nothing, it would explain why I couldn't see it, couldn't even look at it. "So what about the giant spider?"

"I'm getting to that." She held up her left hand, placed her right one flat on top of it. "So somewhere and nowhere. Reality and unreality. Imagine they are stacked, separate layers, with another layer between them."

"Like a cake?"

I swear I could see her trying not to roll her eyes. "Sure, fine. So somewhere and nowhere are like layers of a cake, kept apart by buttercream icing. And there are places where the icing between the layers is thinner. Places where, if you try, you can break through the buttercream."

"I prefer cream cheese icing, personally."

Mercy sighed deeply.

"Sorry," I said quickly. Jokes were just my way of coping. "I think I get it. So the ball pit was a thin place? And when we jumped, we broke through?"

"Yes," she said, then frowned. "Well, no. Actually, there was already a rip in reality. That's why we got through so easily. I'm guessing that kid who went missing must have been the one to break through, though I'm surprised he could manage it."

"Oh, right," I said. "Ronald." I'm ashamed to say I had entirely forgotten about the missing child. That was the reason Mercy had jumped into the ball pit in the first place, wasn't it?

"So that's why there's stuff here, like the trampoline and the spider." Mercy gestured around us. "Once there's a hole, reality leaks in."

"How do you know all this?" I asked.

"It's kind of like a family secret," she said. "Everyone in my family is particularly sensitive to thin places in the world, and we're able to break through them. My mother is always warning me not to go through holes in the world."

Certainly not the sort of thing my mother had ever warned me about.

"She also told me normal people aren't even capable of breaking through on their own," said Mercy, "but I guess that kid must have."

Before I could become too annoyed at my presumed status as a boring "normal" person, the thundering voice sounded in the distance again.

"I think it's coming from over there," Mercy said, pointing. "We should go that way."

Without a moment's hesitation, she jumped off in the direction the voice had come from. Which was brave of her, I guess.

Though according to my mother, the bravest thing of all is when you're super scared of something but you do it anyway.

So I guess I was the brave one when, reluctantly, I followed.

ODD BUT NOT DEAD

W e jumped from trampoline to trampoline and soon I caught sight of something like a forest in the distance. Massive tree trunks, redwood size and clown-red colored. As we got closer, I saw that some of the trunks were blue or green or yellow, and some went sideways instead of up and down.

These were not, in fact, trees, but tubes. Plastic tubes.

It was like this world was pasted together from scraps of the world we'd just left. How had Mercy put it? *Reality leaks in.*

Eventually we came upon a red tube that was open at one end, the hollow plastic gaping like the maw of an enormous beast. There was a space of about a foot between it and the trampoline we stood on.

Mercy leapt and landed neatly inside the tunnel. I hesitated.

"Come on," said Mercy.

"What would happen if I fell into that?" I pointed at the staticky nothingness below us. "Would it kill me?"

"I think you'd be okay," said Mercy, with less confidence than I'd have liked.

"You think? I thought you said you'd been to a place like this before."

"Only sort of," she said. "I got there the same way—breaking through a thin place in the world. But it looked nothing like this." She frowned. "My mother told me that if we could observe Nowhere in its natural state, it would just be absolute nothingness. But we can't, because as soon as a person enters Nowhere, they change it. Substance grows around them the same way a grit in an oyster grows a pearl."

A small part of my brain could acknowledge how cool this all was. *Voidjumper* was real, kind of! A larger part of my brain, however, was still frantically screaming at me that death was imminent. *Run!* it cried. *Hide! Get to safety!* Never mind that safety was a whole world away.

I took a step forward, readying myself to jump across the gap, but froze at the last minute.

"Okay," I said. "Just one more question. Why did your mom warn you not to go through a hole in the world?"

She sighed. "I told you about my allergies, right?"

"I guess. You said you were allergic to everything." I'd thought she'd been joking, honestly.

"I'm allergic to everything real," she clarified. "Runs

in my family. And here, where practically nothing is real, my allergies don't bother me at all. My mother knew if I found my way to Nowhere, I might never want to come back."

"Oh." That wasn't the answer I expected at all. It was reassuring, I guess. Better than: *don't go to Nowhere or you'll die horribly within minutes.*

"And," Mercy added casually, "if a person did stay here too long, the hole in the world would grow and grow until it destroyed all of reality."

With that delightful pronouncement, Mercy turned on her heel and strode down the tunnel away from me. Unlike the real tunnels, this one was large enough for even a tall person to comfortably walk upright. My fear of being left alone overcame my fear of falling endlessly. I took a deep breath, moved back to get a bouncing start, and leapt across the divide.

"You're real," I said to Mercy, once I caught up with her, "aren't you?"

"That's a stupid question."

I would have thought so, too, not very long ago, but now here we were in the middle of literal Nowhere.

"If you're allergic to everything real," I went on, "does that mean you're allergic to yourself?"

Mercy didn't answer. The farther we walked, the darker it got, as the tube twisted and turned away from the entrance. Before long there was no light save a faint reddish glow coming from the occasional joint where one length of plastic tubing had been bolted to another. It was creepy, and I found myself rambling nervously just to fill the silence.

"And like air is real," I said, "so how do you breathe? And food is real, so how do you eat? Or drink? Water is real. The ground is real. And like . . . *toilets* . . . those are real."

"It's not funny," Mercy snapped, turning to face me. "You're right. Everything you listed, we're a little bit allergic to. So it's hard for us to exist. Just being alive is sort of like being stung by bees all the time, okay?"

"Oh," I said, lamely. "Sorry."

We walked in silence for a moment, but then Mercy stopped so suddenly that I nearly ran into her.

"What is it?" I asked. I squeezed up beside her. There was just enough room for us to stand side by side with shoulders touching. I could see now why she had stopped. She'd had no other option. Directly ahead of us the floor itself stopped and the tube took a neat ninety-degree turn straight down.

Mercy knelt at the edge of the drop-off. She pulled a tiny flashlight keychain out of her pocket, which I recognized right away as one of the prizes from the prize counter.

She shone the keychain down the tube. I couldn't see

much. Just a thin beam of light fading off into the darkness.

"It doesn't go straight down," Mercy said. "It curves, like a slide."

"Are you sure?"

"Yes," she said. "Mostly."

"Let me see."

I took the flashlight and leaned over as far as I could without falling.

"It's not as if we've got much of a choice," said Mercy, "unless you want to go back the way we came."

"I can't see anything," I said.

"Doesn't matter. You don't need to see to slide. Go on."

I hesitated.

"What's the matter," said Mercy, "are you scared of slides, too?"

"What? No! Of course not."

I wasn't. Not in the least. Ha! Of course not. Certainly not. Not in the slightest. I was just unsure of how to proceed. Should I jump? Should I sit on the edge and then scoot off? There were just so many decisions, each of which must be carefully weighed. That was all.

Definitely not scared.

"Oh for goodness' sake." Mercy pushed me out of the way and before I could react, she had disappeared down the dark tunnel.

"Mercy," I called. "Mercy! Does it curve?"

There was no answer. I sighed and sat on the floor of the tube with my legs dangling down into the dark of the drop-off. Praying that there'd be a trampoline at the bottom and not a pit of spiders, I took a deep breath and pushed myself off the edge.

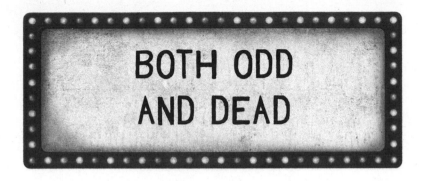

BOTH ODD
AND DEAD

And so I fell, for the second time that day, although it was not like that first time.

No, this time it was worse.

This time, I was expecting it. I'd begun to panic even before my feet left solid ground. I freaked out and tried to grab onto the sides of the tube, my fingers scrabbling uselessly at the slick plastic.

My left shoulder slammed against the wall of the tube. I was knocked across to the opposite wall, onto my back. Then, just as Mercy had said, I found that I was no longer falling but sliding. The curve was slight, the angle steep, and I was sliding very fast, but I was sliding. The friction of my back and legs against the plastic burned.

I heard a crash from below me. A moment later, the tube ended, and I flew through the air. Mercy must have had the foresight to roll out of the way when she landed so I wouldn't fall on top of her, which was lucky for her, but unfortunate for me. What I landed on instead was anything but soft. After the initial shock of impact wore off, I became aware of what felt like a thousand tiny knives digging into my back.

"Augghh!" I said, and also, "Eeeuurrgghh!"

It was pitch-dark here. I could hear Mercy moving around next to me, but I couldn't see her.

Suddenly, a bright light flooded my field of vision. I shielded my eyes, although not quite fast enough.

Peering through the cracks between my fingers, I could see that I had landed on a pile of glimmering jewels. I picked one up to get a better look.

"John?" said Mercy.

"Huh?" I said. I pulled my hand away from my face and sat up. Now that my eyes had adjusted to the light, I noticed several things.

First, the object I was holding was not a jewel after all, but a plastic ring. The colored plastic was translucent, slightly iridescent, and molded to imitate the angular cuts of a diamond—exactly the sort of junk stocked at the Krazyland prize counter.

Second, we were currently sitting in a small room, about the size of my bedroom at home, with curved red walls and circular doors.

Third, next to one of the doors in the far wall there was a light switch and next to that light switch stood a middle-aged man.

"Mercy?" said the man. "Is that you?"

"It's me," said Mercy. She got to her feet and brushed herself off before helping me up. "Nathan this is John, the former chief of security. John, this is Nathan, Steven's nephew."

As she spoke, John picked his way carefully across the floor, now littered with all the plastic rings that had scattered when we fell. I could see that he was indeed wearing the classic dark blue uniform of a security guard. His hair was mostly gray, and his skin was heavily lined. He took a good look at Mercy.

"Well, knock me over with a feather," he said. "It really is you." He put a hand to his chest and hung his head. "You're both so young. The world is unfair."

"Mr. Clark was furious after you disappeared," Mercy told him. Clark was Uncle Steven's last name.

"Disappeared?" asked John, giving her a curious look.

"Yeah. He thought you'd skipped town. But I guess you just came here. That explains some things."

"I don't understand." John frowned. "Didn't he find the body?"

"Hold up now," I cut in. "Slow down. You used to work at Krazyland? And then you disappeared? And now you're here."

"Right on two counts," said John. "But I'm sorry to say, young man—I didn't disappear, I died."

DEATH IS LIKE
A DISCOUNT SPA

John insisted we come in and sit down, so Mercy and I followed him through one of the round doors into a larger room, which held rows and rows of Lava lamps, a heap of tangled Slinkys, and at least two dozen boxes of bouncy balls. Stacked up in one corner were a bunch of blow-up chairs in various colors. John pulled out three and set them on the floor.

"So," he said. "This is a bit awkward."

"You're not dead," said Mercy.

"I am," said John. His face fell. "And I'm afraid that you two must be as well."

A brief stab of fear shot through me. I didn't feel dead, but I'd never actually been dead before, so I couldn't be sure. Maybe being dead just felt like being alive, only weirder.

"We're not dead," said Mercy.

"I believe you're experiencing denial," said John gently. "It's the first stage of grief."

"I'm not dead," insisted Mercy. "Nobody here is dead."

"I know it's a lot to take in," said John, "but it's really not so bad, being dead. Honestly, it's quite peaceful."

At that point the floor shook and the roar of the voice sounded, muffled, in the distance. A few boxes tumbled down from their stacks, releasing a flood of bouncy balls in every color and glitter-level imaginable.

"Well, usually it's peaceful," John amended. He got up and started righting the fallen boxes. "Honestly, though, I can't complain. I get plenty of time to relax. I've taken up collecting."

"I don't understand," I said to John, which was an understatement. "How did you die?"

"He didn't," Mercy cut in.

"Well, okay, how do you *think* you died?"

"The old ticker," John answered. He was gathering up the scattered bouncy balls. Mercy and I knelt to help him.

"Like a heart attack, you mean?" I asked.

"Right you are," said John. "I was locking the place up for the night when I thought I heard something rustling in the big ball pit. I figured a raccoon had gotten in again."

I wasn't sure if I'd heard him right. *Again?*

"So I waded in there to try and flush the thing out,"

he continued, before I could worry further about the raccoon-based revelation. "But wouldn't you know it my heart chose that exact moment to give up the ghost, if you'll excuse the expression. Not the worst way to go. I'm just sorry for whoever found me."

"Nobody found you," said Mercy, sounding exasperated. "You didn't die."

John shrugged. "Well, then how do you account for the angels?"

"Do these angels happen to have eight legs?" I asked.

"Certainly not. You'll see. Wait around long enough and one will show. They usually come through there." He pointed to a round door set into the wall opposite.

I glanced over at Mercy, expecting her to argue. But she'd gone quiet. She was holding a glittery bouncy ball and gazing at it as if it were in fact a diminutive crystal ball.

"This is real," she said. She held it out to me. "It must have fallen through, too."

I took it, rolled it around my palm. "How can you tell?"

"It's obvious." She tossed me another ball. "See, this one isn't real."

I compared the two. The pattern of colored swirls varied slightly, but that was it.

"They look the same," I said.

She shrugged. "Smell them."

Feeling ridiculous, I held one to my nose and sniffed.

It had no scent, but it was a bouncy ball not a rose. Worried this was a prank, I sniffed the other one.

"Oh," I said. It was faint, but there. A slight rubbery scent.

Mercy smiled triumphantly. "The smell of reality. Haven't you noticed that everything here smells wrong?"

I shook my head.

"Nowhere can't create anything new," she explained. "It can only copy things that already exist, but it tends to get the details wrong. Like smells, for instance. It's the same with people." She gestured toward John, who looked embarrassed.

"The afterlife," he admitted, "does not have showers."

"I don't mean you smell bad," said Mercy. "But fake people don't smell like anything. There's other little things they tend to get wrong—breathing, blinking."

John blinked at her. "Are *you* angels? You are a bit more solid than the others, but I suppose you could be."

"Wait," I said, thoroughly lost. "There's fake people?"

"Of course," said Mercy. "This place is copying Krazyland." She gestured at the giant plastic tube in which we sat, the prize-counter junk. "And Krazyland has people in it, too. Kids and parents and your uncle and us."

"I'm afraid I don't follow," said John.

"I can explain later. Right now, we need to find this missing kid. Have you seen him?" Mercy gave John a brief description of Ronald.

His face lit up. "Oh yes, he passed by here not that long ago."

"Where did he go?"

John pointed to a round door, the same one he'd said the angels came through.

Mercy strode over and pulled it open. Beyond was a blue tunnel that sloped gently upward.

"Are you coming with us?" Mercy asked John.

Before he could answer, the voice thundered in the distance, clearly coming from the direction we were about to go.

John's face fell. "I didn't want to alarm you, but I've been warned not to go that way. There are some parts of the afterlife that aren't so peaceful."

"We'll come back for you," said Mercy, and without waiting for a response, she clambered up the blue tunnel and out of sight.

SHADOW

I clambered after Mercy, though John's words lingered in my mind. He'd been warned? By who?

As we went, the slope of the tunnel grew steeper, and my socks started to slip on the plastic. I had to shout to Mercy, who was way ahead of me, to wait up a second so I could take them off. Mercy had taken off her socks, too. Our shoes were back in the real world, presumably having a nice, normal time.

It was easier to walk in bare feet, but it was still a difficult climb. The tunnel just kept getting steeper, and it wasn't long before I was out of breath.

"Wait," I shouted again to Mercy, who was so far above me I could only see her feet. She stuck her head back down to look at me.

"It ends up here," she said. "There's some kind of room."

I took a deep breath and, with my muscles crying out for me to stop, pulled myself the rest of the way up. About twenty feet above where I'd been, the tunnel opened up into what could, indeed, be called some kind of room.

It was spherical and very large. There were no piles of plastic junk littering the floor. Instead, there were tunnels, dozens of them, branching off in every direction. Light came from the entrances to some. Others were dark. It was like a train station, or a hive.

"We really aren't dead, right?" I asked Mercy.

"Definitely not," she said. "John must have been the one who broke through first. No wonder everything is so overgrown."

"Overgrown?" It seemed a funny way to describe it, like a garden gone untended.

"Yeah," she said. "He disappeared months ago, which means reality must have been leaking in that whole time."

"Is that—?" I started to ask, but before I could say *bad,* Mercy cut me off.

"Shhhh," she hissed. "Someone's coming."

We both got very quiet. After a few moments, I heard it, too: the faint sound of footsteps. I couldn't tell which tunnel it was coming from.

Mercy and I waited in silence. The footsteps grew louder.

I inched backward, trying to stay calm and failing.

A shadow appeared at the mouth of a yellow tunnel to our left. I inched farther back. The shadow shortened, became more defined.

I peered around Mercy, who I may or may not have been hiding behind. The owner of the shadow hopped down from the end of the yellow tunnel into the big room.

It was a child, perhaps six or seven. He stopped when he saw us and stared. I stared back.

This clearly wasn't Ronald. His shirt wasn't red.

Also he was completely transparent.

I could see right through him. I could see the floor through his shoes and the tunnels behind him through his shirt. Even his face was more like a window than a wall.

"Hello," said Mercy, apparently unfazed.

"Hi," said the see-through kid. He looked between the two of us. "Um, I'm not in trouble, am I?"

"Of course not," said Mercy.

"Only I couldn't think of any more stories to tell her," he said. "So I runned off. If I remember more, I'll go back."

"Tell who?" I asked.

He gave me a look like I was the stupidest person who ever lived. This kid could be Mercy's understudy. "Big Bertha," he said.

As if on cue, the thundering voice sounded. It echoed through the chamber. The kid scampered off down another tunnel.

"He was fake?" I asked. I'd been too distracted to notice if he'd smelled weird or blinked enough or anything like that.

There had been that one other clue, though. Fairly hard to miss.

"Yeah." Mercy walked over to the yellow tunnel he'd first come from and peered down it. "We should probably go this way."

The yellow tunnel seemed, much to my relief, basically level. I climbed in. A tremor ran through the plastic under my feet. It lasted only for a second, maybe two. From somewhere down the tunnel, I heard the low rumble of the voice calling out for more.

I would have loved to turn around and run away like the see-through kid, but Mercy already thought little enough of me as it was. Heroically, nobly, practically sweating charm and bravery, I strode forward.

"Why was that kid transparent?" I asked as we walked. "The giant spider wasn't see-through."

Mercy considered this for a moment. "You know how way back in the early nineteen hundreds they had these cameras with really long exposure times, so it would take like five minutes to take one picture?"

"I guess," I said, though I had no idea what that had to do with anything.

"Let's say the two of us were posing for a picture," she continued, "and I stood still the whole time but you just ran through. When the photo was developed, I'd look solid and you'd look all ghostly. I think it's like that. Nowhere is sort of trying to take a picture of the real world.

The machines and the play structures are there all the time, but the kids just come in for an hour or two and then leave."

"Right," I said, "makes sense." But I was lying. It didn't make sense at all. Nothing did anymore.

We'd been walking for maybe five minutes—I tried to check my animal watch, but the hands weren't moving—when we reached the end of the tunnel. The voice had boomed out several more times. It seemed to be growing in both frequency and volume. I speed-walked ahead, eager to show that I was not afraid. So I was the first one to step from the yellow tube into a wide open space full of bright light.

And I was the first one to lay my eyes on *her*.

STORY TIME

The room we entered was at least twice the size of my high school gym, with a ceiling that curved up into a cathedral dome.

Bertha sat in the center of the room, yarn hair nearly brushing the rafters, red-and-white polka-dot sack dress spread out around her like a circus tent. She had to be at least twenty feet tall. Her head was almost half the size of her body, and her mouth, outlined in thick red lipstick, took up most of her head.

It was not her size, though, that made me stop in my tracks.

Back in the real world, Bertha was just a bit of cloth in a cabinet. Her eyes were flat plastic. She couldn't move, except in a few jerky, mechanical patterns.

Here, she was unmistakably alive. Her shiny black eyes, each the size of my whole head, roamed the room.

She lifted a fabric hand to brush a strand of yarn hair out of her face.

Mercy stepped out of the tunnel behind me. "Wow," she said, which was an understatement.

"MORE," said Bertha. Her voice echoed off the walls and shook my bones. When she opened her mouth, I saw that she had teeth.

Arrayed around Bertha, standing on the floor or sitting, was a crowd of transparent children—fake children. To Bertha's left, two kids were standing atop a netting scaffold. One was translucent, like the kid we'd seen earlier, but the other . . .

I grabbed Mercy's arm. "Look, he's got a red shirt. And he's not see-through!"

The kid, who had to be Ronald, stepped forward.

"Um," he said, "so this one time me and my older brother went to the lake and we wanted to catch fish but we didn't have any stuff with us so we tied some vines to sticks and tried to fish with that but we didn't catch nothing. So then we went to this shallow part and there was these little tiny fish . . ."

As he spoke, a strange thing began to shimmer in the air. At first it was formless, just a small cloud that had lost its way and wandered into a room. But as he went on, the cloud drew itself together into shapes—small fish, darting here and there through the air.

"And so then we tried to catch 'em with our hands," Ronald went on, "but they kept slipping away."

"Tell me more," said Bertha, her voice a subdued rumble now, instead of a shout. "What did these fish look like?"

"Well, they were no bigger than, um, maybe a fingernail or a paperclip. And they were all silvery like paperclips, too."

The fish in the air shivered for a moment into the shape of swimming fingernails—which was a bit grisly—and then paperclips, and then back into fish. Sunlight with no clear source shone on the scene. Ghostly hands grasped at the tiny fish.

Bertha reached out, grabbed the whole shimmering image, and popped it into her mouth. She closed her eyes, as if savoring it, chewed, swallowed.

The fake children in the room all clapped.

"What's going on?" I whispered to Mercy.

"I'm not sure," she said. "We have to get him out of here somehow, though."

Mercy began to inch her way along the wall toward the scaffolding.

Bertha opened her eyes. Mercy froze.

"That one was so fresh," said Bertha, "so vivid. Tell me another, child."

"I'm tired of stories," said Ronald. "I want to go jump on the trampolines some more."

"I'm hungry," Bertha said. "I need more."

"Go on," said the other transparent kid on the scaffold, nudging Ronald.

"You do one." Ronald nudged him back.

"MORE," demanded Bertha.

"Fine," said the transparent kid. "So once upon a time my aunt Ruth took me to Krazyland—"

Bertha cut him off. "You've already told this one."

Ronald hopped down from the scaffolding. Mercy was still inching toward him. I watched, holding my breath, too afraid to follow.

"Okay," the transparent kid said, "so this one time I got a pizza at Krazyland and all the cheese fell off."

"No," said Bertha, "you've told this one, too."

Ronald was headed toward another tunnel opening on the wall opposite us. Bertha wasn't paying him any attention, but Mercy was still going slowly along the wall. He would probably escape down a tunnel before she caught up to him. I took a deep breath, steeled myself. If I ran straight forward, I could reach him.

"Um," said the transparent kid, "once I was in the ball pit at Krazyland and—"

"NO." Bertha cut him off. The room shook and I froze. "I've heard all of these before." She pointed an enormous finger accusingly at the transparent kid.

He just shrugged. "That's all I can remember."

Bertha sighed. Then she reached down, plucked him

up between her thumb and forefinger just as easily as if
he were a bit of pocket lint, raised him high in the air,
his legs kicking at nothing, and dropped him down her
throat.

"MORE," she said.

SNACK TIME

The kids in the room scattered, shrieking.

I lost track of Ronald in the sudden rush, but I ran forward anyway.

"MORE," shouted Bertha. Her glistening black eyes roamed the room. She reached for one fake child and then another, but they all dove out of the way at the last moment, like a bizarre life-size game of Whac-A-Mole.

I finally spotted Ronald again all the way on the other side of the room, about to dart down a tunnel.

"Ronald!" I shouted.

He turned, which gave me just enough time to catch up to him and grab his arm.

"Who are you?" he asked.

"Nathan. From the real world. I'm here to save you!"

With a deft motion, he twisted out of my grasp and lunged away to the side. Luckily, Mercy was there to catch him.

"Come on," she said, and dragged him back across the room, weaving her way nimbly between the fake children, who still ran to and fro, shrieking at the top of their transparent lungs.

I started to follow but stopped short when I spotted a man stepping out of a tunnel on the far side of the room. He wasn't transparent. There was something familiar about him, too. He had a long gray beard, round colored glasses.

It took me a moment, but then it hit me. He was the old man—the one who had handed me a stuffed frog all those years ago. Mercy's grandfather.

I shouted for Mercy, but she must not have heard me over the din, because she hopped into the tunnel we'd come from, still dragging Ronald, and was gone.

"What's all this noise," demanded the man who seemed to be Mercy's grandfather. He stood staring up at Bertha with his arms crossed. "Keep it down out here."

"MORE," Bertha repeated, even louder than before. The floor shuddered beneath my feet. I felt my heart skip a beat.

"I've told you all my stories twenty times," he said. "You can't always be hungry. Real people aren't always hungry, you know."

Bertha scowled down at him. Then she reached out, grabbed him, and popped him into her mouth.

I clapped a hand over my own mouth to keep myself from crying out.

"MORE," Bertha cried.

I stood, stunned for a moment, children in varying degrees of opacity streaming past me in all directions.

A shadow fell across me. I looked up to see Big Bertha's hand hovering above my head like a five-fingered storm cloud.

I turned and ran like hell.

GHOST AND ANGELS WITH WHIPPED CREAM ON TOP

I caught up with Mercy in the spherical hive room. She still had a firm grip on Ronald's arm. He appeared to be sulking.

"Oh good," she said when she saw me. "I was worried you got eaten."

She didn't sound that worried, but I decided not to mention it.

"That was worse than the spiders," I said.

Mercy nodded. "She was . . . well, honestly I wasn't expecting any of that. I think this place has existed for too long. It's gotten too wild. We need to get John and this kid back to the real world right away."

"No!" shouted Ronald, and with a sudden wriggle, he slipped away from Mercy's grasp. He bolted for the nearest tunnel. Mercy and I both tried to block him but ended up knocking into each other. Ronald dove down the tunnel and I just barely managed to grab his ankle in time.

"Where are you going?" I demanded.

"I don't want to go back," he whined, trying to kick me away as I hauled him back into the room with us. "The real world is boring."

I shot Mercy a look of desperation. She just shrugged. "He's right, it is."

I gave a silent apology to the universe for every time in my life I'd complained about being bored. Boring was fine. Boring was safe. Take me back to boring, back to my room, where I could shut the door against the whole world.

"Your parents are really worried about you," I told Ronald. He just stuck out his tongue at me and continued trying to escape my grasp.

"Boring or not," Mercy conceded, "we do need to get all the real people out of here as soon as we can. It's the only way that the hole in the world will heal."

"What if we buy you ice cream?" I asked Ronald.

He stopped struggling. "What kind?'

"What kind do you want?"

"Triple fudge sundae with sprinkles and whipped cream."

"Deal." It was a bluff. I had no intention of buying this brat anything. I didn't have any money, anyway.

Ronald nodded, apparently satisfied. I let go of his foot but kept an eye on him.

"Okay," said Mercy. "Let's hurry."

"Wait," I said. "What if there's other real people here?"

"I think we would have noticed if any other kids fell through."

"I, well, I saw someone. . . ." I hesitated. Her grandfather was dead, wasn't he? Jake had confirmed that. Did ghosts exist in Nowhere? Anything seemed possible now. "Maybe he was fake, but he wasn't transparent like the kids. He, uh, he looked like the guy who used to run Krazyland before: your grandfather."

Mercy frowned at me. "That's not a very nice joke."

"I'm sorry, it's not a joke! I saw him."

She shook her head. "It can't have been him, not even a copy of him. If John is the one who first fell through, then this place has only existed for a few months. My grandfather died two years ago. You must be mistaken. Come on."

She jumped down the tunnel that led to John's place. I glared at Ronald until he slid down, too, and then I followed.

When we reached the room at the end of the tunnel, Mercy shouted for John. A few seconds later he came shuffling out of the door to the left.

"Oh!" he cried. "I'm glad you made it back in one piece. And I see you've found the angel you were looking for."

"What?" I said.

"He means him," said Mercy, pointing at Ronald, who had already managed to pry open one of the boxes of bouncy balls and was testing them to see which one bounced the highest.

I was confused for a moment but then it dawned on me. Earlier, John had said we seemed *more solid than the others*. When he first arrived in this place, he must have met some of the fake kids and assumed that their peculiar appearance meant they were heavenly beings.

"Do you know a guy with a gray beard and round glasses?" I asked John. Maybe he could confirm whether the man I'd seen had actually been Mercy's grandfather.

Mercy shot me an angry look. Ronald bounced a neon green ball, which ricocheted off the ceiling and hit me in the face.

"Of course," said John. "My old boss. Regrettably, he preceded me to this afterlife, but he showed me the ropes when he arrived. He was the one who warned me not to go that way."

John pointed to the tunnel we'd just come from.

"Never mind that," said Mercy, waving a dismissive hand. "We need some way to get to the giant cloud of balls in the sky." She said it as if that were a totally normal and reasonable need.

John beamed. "I've got just the thing."

WEIRDEST AIRLINE EVER

John led us into another room with curving plastic walls. It, too, was filled to the brim with prize-counter junk. He pointed out a large inflatable bear in one corner. I recognized it immediately as the same one Mercy had been using as a pillow the other day.

Well, it probably wasn't the exact same one, but a copy. This one seemed even larger than the real one, but otherwise it looked identical.

"There you go," said John.

I was about to ask what he meant when the bear turned its head and looked at me. I yelped and jumped back. That was not right.

"Cool," said Ronald.

The bear opened its mouth and flashed a row of sharp teeth. That was not right at all.

"Now, now," said John, seemingly addressing the bear. "None of that. These are my friends."

The bear made a huffing noise. It climbed slowly to its feet.

"How is this going to help?" Mercy asked.

Seemingly in response, the bear tensed and then jumped toward us. I scrambled back so fast that I fell on my butt.

The bear, however, did not come crashing down upon me teeth first, but rather stopped in midair and floated, hovering just above our heads.

"Super cool!" said Ronald.

"Oh," said Mercy. "I see."

"There should be a few more of them around here." John put two fingers to his lips and gave a shrill whistle, as though he were calling a dog.

I racked my brains trying to remember what other inflatable animals the prize counter stocked. They were in the mid-tier of prizes, above all the plastic junk but not worth quite as many tickets as the electronics. Was there a cat maybe?

I got my answer a moment later when a hot pink lion with an orange mane came sauntering through the door. It stretched and yawned, revealing—you guessed it— gleaming rows of teeth.

The teeth were probably just plastic filled with air, but they sure looked sharp and I wasn't about to take my chances.

Mercy, however, walked right over and started petting the lion. It made a weird sort of noise that I think was purring, or possibly a hairball. An airball? Really, I found the fact that it could make any kind of sound at all mysterious enough.

Behind the lion, an inflatable giraffe was ducking through the door, long neck bent low.

"Dibs on the giraffe," I said quickly. As long as I made sure not to look like the top of a tree, perhaps I could survive.

John ushered us and the animals down another tunnel, which stopped about twenty feet in and opened onto the sky—if it was indeed the sky and not just some abstract concept of a sky held aloft by wishful thinking.

"Okay," said Mercy, "I'll take the lion and Ronald can ride with me. Nathan can take the giraffe. John, you take the bear."

"I'd really better stay and keep—" John started, but Mercy didn't let him finish.

"No." She turned sharply, glaring at him. "You can't stay. You're coming with us. Nobody real can stay here."

I thought again of the man I'd seen back with Bertha—in the moment I'd been sure he must be real, but now I felt less certain. I tried to push the incident from my mind. We were going home. Everything would be okay once we got back to the real world, to safety.

"Well, all right," said John, though he looked doubtful. "I suppose I can leave my collection unattended for a little while."

Mercy swung herself onto the lion's back and helped Ronald up. The lion sauntered out the end of the tunnel and straight into the middle of the air, where it continued as if nothing whatsoever had changed.

As for the giraffe, I wouldn't have felt truly comfortable unless it was made of airtight Kevlar with triple layering and a dozen back-up parachutes. Heck, even then I would be less than enthusiastic. Still, against my better judgment, I climbed aboard.

The giraffe walked slowly to the end of the tunnel. I squeezed my eyes shut.

I felt when it stepped off the edge. My heart dropped into my lower intestine, but the giraffe merely gave a slight bobble and then kept going.

I opened my eyes.

This isn't so bad, I thought to myself. I could get used to this.

Then I looked down.

WORST AIRLINE EVER

There was nothing below us.

I don't just mean it was a long way to the ground. There was no ground. Only a terrifying nothingness, which my eyes skidded across in a panicked rush, desperate to find anything to focus on. The nothingness didn't look like darkness or light. It had no color, no texture. It gave me an instant headache as my brain tried fruitlessly to process what my eyes weren't seeing.

What would happen if I fell into that? Would I cease to exist? Even Mercy didn't know.

I focused on my hands, which were gripping the giraffe's neck so tightly I was terrified it would pop. I tried to keep my grip light and my thoughts buoyant, though I could feel my heart pounding faster and faster.

"You need to head upward," Mercy shouted down at me.

Mercy's lion cavorted above me, swooping and swerving through the air. Ronald whooped with delight.

The giraffe continued to plod straight forward at a pace which, clocking in somewhere between a lazy snail and moss growing on the trunk of a tree, was still several times too fast for my comfort.

"Uh, giddy up," I suggested to the giraffe. "Mush."

The giraffe twitched its plastic ears a few times but otherwise didn't react.

There was something ahead of us now. Something enormous.

It rose out of the nothingness like a mountain rising through mist. And perhaps it was a mountain, though a very odd-looking one, smooth and impossibly steep with perfectly straight edges.

"Come on," shouted Mercy. She circled around and swooped down behind me. The lion, seeming to pick up on her mood, opened its mouth and roared at me.

That finally got through to the giraffe, which abruptly stopped and twisted its long neck around to see what was going on. I felt myself begin to unbalance and was forced to throw my arms around its neck.

I heard Mercy swear and turned in time to see the lion leaping toward me and the giraffe, claws outstretched. The giraffe made a guttural noise and swung its enormous neck at the lion.

The two met midair. I clung on for dear life as the giraffe twisted and bucked. John was steering the bear toward us, which seemed like it would only make things worse.

"Call your lion off!" I shouted to Mercy.

"I'm trying!" she shouted back.

The giraffe managed to knock the lion aside, but the lion circled around for another attack. It opened its jaws and clamped down hard upon one of the giraffe's long spindly legs.

I heard a sickening pop followed by the hiss of released air.

The giraffe and I began to plummet. I could feel it deflating beneath me. The neck flopped loose, twisting in the breeze. I squeezed my eyes shut.

ISAAC NEWTON WAS WRONG

I would like to state, for the record, that I neither screamed nor fainted nor wet myself at this juncture. Probably I had gone into shock.

The giraffe had just enough air left in it to cushion my fall as we slammed into the ground.

Later, it would occur to me that I should be thankful there had been something beneath us to land on at all, but at that moment I simply lay stunned.

The lion swooped down, with the bear following a moment later.

Shakily, I climbed to my feet, disentangling myself from the deflated giraffe. I'd landed at the foot of the strange mountain. The ground beneath my feet was smooth and shiny, like polished wood.

The lion landed gracefully beside me. The bear plopped down a few feet away and immediately curled up and went to sleep.

Mercy slid off the lion's back. "What did you do?" she asked.

"Me?! Nothing. It was your stupid lion."

"Is it dead?" Ronald asked from his perch on the culprit's back.

Mercy crouched down to get a better look at the puddle of plastic that had been the giraffe. "Maybe we can reinflate it somehow."

The giraffe, to my great surprise, picked up its head to look at her. A head that was, mind you, basically two-dimensional now, completely devoid of air. The expression on the deflated face was somehow disapproving.

With a sudden lurch, the giraffe turned and slithered along the ground like a weirdly shaped snake.

"Hey!" I shouted, "wait!" But it did not. It slithered right up the sheer slope and disappeared into a dark, circular chasm near the top—some kind of cave, I supposed.

John stood nearby with his hand on his hip, surveying the slope.

"Ah," he said, "one of the angels told me about this place, though I'd never seen it myself. These must be the Skee-Ball mountains."

The mountain did, in fact, resemble a giant Skee-Ball lane. What I had taken for round caves at the top were, I realized, the scoring holes.

As I was taking this in, the ground shook beneath our feet.

The lion sprang into the air, Ronald tumbling from its back. I just had time to glance behind us before three enormous boulders rolled by, one of them passing within inches of me.

The boulders continued, improbably, up the sheer slope ahead of us, seeming to gather speed even as they rolled directly upward.

At the top they disappeared into the circular caves.

"The angel mentioned that, too," John said. "Told me you have to watch out for the reverse avalanches."

"You know they aren't angels, right?" said Mercy. "Just kids."

John shrugged.

"Where's the bear?" asked Ronald.

We all spun around, searching, until Mercy spotted it far in the distance, hightailing it away. The lion, too, had flown off and abandoned us.

"What do we do now?" I asked.

"We could try to climb," said Mercy, pointing up. At its peak, the mountain almost reached the cloud of plastic balls.

"It doesn't look very climbable," said John.

Ronald was in fact already engaged in trying to do just that. The surface of the Skee-Ball lanes was too slick, the slope too steep. Even with bare feet, he couldn't get more than a few feet up. A few moments later, the shaking came again. We were all prepared this time, dropping to the ground before the next round of boulders came whiz-zing past.

"They get to the top somehow," I pointed out.

"Let's see where they're coming from," said Mercy.

We headed in the opposite direction of the slope. The flat part of the track, where we were, stretched on for a long time, but finally we came to the end.

Set into the ground here was a large circular pit. Cautiously, I peered in. It was dark in there, distinctly cave-like. The walls seemed to be stone, and heavily shadowed.

Mercy ushered us to either side, so we'd be out of immediate danger.

When the next boulder appeared, we could observe how it simply popped straight up out of the ground and went hurtling up the mountain.

"I have a theory," said Mercy. She approached the pit again and peered in. "Let's wait for the next ones."

I inched up next to her and stared down into the darkness. It reminded me a little of the void. But there were no stars. Besides, if this were *Voidjumper,* it would have been much easier to leave.

"Whatcha going to do?" asked Ronald.

"Are you old enough to know what gravitational force is?" Mercy asked.

He stuck out his tongue at her. "Duh, I'm in third grade."

"Well—"

Her next words were cut off by the shaking and a rumbling noise, which clearly originated from deep within the pit.

She turned to me. "I'm sorry," she shouted.

"What?" I shouted back. "Why?"

And then she pushed me.

THE SMELL OF REALITY

I pitched forward into the cave, but not very far. As luck would have it, there was a speeding boulder there to catch my fall.

It slammed into me, and suddenly I was flying, right back out the way I'd come.

I caught a brief glimpse of the others who seemed, from my perspective, to be standing above me, and then I was falling again. Not back into the cave. No, I was somehow falling up the mountain.

Except it didn't feel like up. And it didn't look like a mountain anymore, but an enormous slide, stretching out below me. The cloud, too, no longer looked like a cloud so much as an ocean. I was falling straight toward it.

I hit the surface of the cloud with a *whumpf* and kept falling. The plastic balls pummeled me from every direction. One hit me right in the eye. Another in a place which I will not mention. The irony did not go unnoticed. Neither did the pain.

Finally, the friction slowed my momentum, and I drifted almost to a stop. I flailed around wildly until my hand brushed up against something—netting.

I was incredibly dizzy by then, and deeply unsure of which way was up, but I kicked my legs out and tried to stand.

My head broke the surface of the ball pit. I gasped for air as if I had been drowning.

It was dark. As my eyes adjusted, I could make out the shape of the foam stairs. I flung myself toward them, wading through the plastic balls.

I collapsed on the steps, breathing heavily, but overcome, too, with relief. A red exit sign floated eerily in the distance.

I was back.

A moment later I heard the plastic balls rustling, and then Mercy's voice.

"Did everyone make it?" she asked.

More rustling. I heard Ronald's voice calling, "I can't see," and then a groan that I thought must be John.

I rolled myself down the steps. My shoes were sitting there on the floor where I'd left them. The sight of them— their sheer boring normalness—almost made me cry. They were scuffed, the laces frayed. But they were distinctly NOT being worn by a giant spider.

And they smelled like feet. Mercy had been right about the smells. It was easier to notice their presence now than their absence before.

"Nathan?" called Mercy.

"I'm dead," I said. "I didn't make it. Tell my parents I loved them."

The thin beam of her keychain flashlight fell across my face. She was crouching on the foam steps, staring down at me.

"You aren't dead," she said, and I could have sworn there was a hint of disappointment in her tone. I don't know, maybe I was imagining it. Maybe not. She had, after all, just pushed me off the equivalent of a cliff without so much as a thought for my emotional or physical well-being.

"Thank goodness that worked," Mercy went on.

"What?!" I sputtered, sitting up. "You weren't sure it was going to work?"

"It was an educated guess," said Mercy.

"It was attempted murder," I countered.

"I don't know what you're so upset about," she said. "We're here, aren't we? Gravity there obviously doesn't follow normal rules. The boulders reversed it."

We turned back toward the ball pit. Ronald was splashing about. John was leaning heavily against one of the mesh walls, hand to his chest. He looked like he might be having a heart attack for real.

"You okay?" Mercy asked.

"Everything's so heavy here," he said. "I'd forgotten what if felt like to be alive."

Mercy waded back in to help him out.

"Do you see now that you weren't dead?" she asked, as they descended the foam steps out of the pit. Ronald scrambled out after them.

John shook his head. "I've been given a second chance at life. I'm a lucky man all right. I won't waste it."

Mercy shrugged. She let Ronald hold the flashlight and the four of us shuffled and stumbled our way out of the maze that was Krazyland Kids Indoor Playplace. It was clearly closed for the day, but as we neared the front, I could see that it was still daylight. How long had we been gone?

When we finally found the door and got outside, I took a deep breath.

"The air," I said. "It really does smell different here." Sort of like stale French fries and rotting cheese. Though perhaps that was less the smell of reality than of the dumpster behind the fast-food place next door. Maybe they were one and the same.

"Told you," said Mercy, stifling a yawn.

AND EVERYTHING WAS SOLVED AND EVERYBODY LIVED HAPPILY EVER AFTER

It was a great comfort, to see the blue sky above us dotted with fluffy white clouds instead of plastic balls. I was feeling exhausted now, too, though apparently not quite so tired as Mercy, who was struggling to keep her eyes open. John was staring in awe at the world around him.

"It's so beautiful," he said. "I never appreciated it, the first time around."

"What do we do now?" I asked.

"I guess we'd better get him home," said Mercy, gesturing at Ronald, who was crouched on the pavement dropping pebbles down a storm drain.

"Hey," said Ronald, straightening up with a scowl. He pointed an accusing finger in my direction. "You promised ice cream."

Mercy sat down on the curb with a sigh.

"I'm sure your parents will get you ice cream," I said.

"You promised!" said Ronald.

I looked down at Mercy, hoping she would back me up. She was slumped over with her head on her knees.

"Mercy!" I crouched and shook her by the shoulders.

She bolted upright and fixed me with a piercing glare.

"I was trying to sleep," she said.

"I'm not going anywhere unless I get ice cream," Ronald insisted, crossing his arms.

"Ice cream," said John dreamily. "I can't remember the last time I had ice cream. Nothing has any taste, you know, when you're dead."

About five minutes later we were all standing by the human-size light-up ice-cream cone in front of the Super Freeze two blocks from Krazyland.

"I want a triple fudge sundae with sprinkles and whipped cream like you promised," said Ronald.

"Sure," I said. "Whatever. Just make sure to tell them you're lost and you need somebody to call your parents."

John produced a crumpled ten-dollar bill from his pocket. Ronald grabbed it and ran across the parking lot to the Super Freeze.

"I bet Mr. Clark would give you your old job back if you wanted," Mercy said to John, "although I'm not sure how you'll explain where you've been."

He shook his head. "I'm going to make the most of this second chance. First thing I want to do is head straight to the bus station and get a ticket out of here. I've got family down in Florida. Some time on a beach would suit me, I think. Do you kids need any help?"

"We'll be okay," I said. I hoped that was true.

"Good luck," said Mercy.

"I'll send you a postcard," John called as he headed down the street.

Somebody's phone started buzzing. I thought it was mine, until I remembered that my phone was hopelessly lost. Mercy pulled hers from her pocket and answered.

My uncle's voice came through so loud I could hear it.

"Mercy!" he shouted. "Are you okay? Is Nathan there with you?"

She glanced at me. "Yes, he's here."

"Where are you? What happened? I've been driving all over town looking for you two."

"Um," said Mercy. She gave me a look of utter bafflement.

"Here," I said, "let me talk to him." I was good at talking to grown-ups. Arguably better than I was at talking to kids my own age.

Mercy handed the phone over but not before muffling it with a hand and whispering: "You can't tell him what really happened. He'll think we're making it up."

I nodded. The trick to successful lying, I'd found, was to tell the truth, just not all of it.

"Hey," I said to my uncle. "We found that kid Ronald."

"You did? Where?"

"He wanted ice cream." Technically true.

"Ice cream?"

"Yeah, he's at the Super Freeze. Looks like his parents are pulling up now." Also true. A station wagon had just veered into the lot and parked sloppily across two spaces.

"Oh, thank goodness," said Uncle Steven. "That's a huge relief. Wait there, I'll come pick you up."

I hung up and watched Ronald's parents as they ran into the Super Freeze.

"Did that all really happen?" I asked Mercy. "I mean the spiders and Bertha and all that?"

But she didn't answer. While I'd been talking on the phone, she'd leaned against the giant plastic ice-cream cone and fallen asleep.

OR NOT

Uncle Steven arrived soon after and hustled us into his car. Mercy fell asleep again almost immediately, head hanging down to her chest, kept upright only by her seatbelt.

There were so many things I wanted to ask her, but I couldn't with my uncle there. He was asking *me* questions, trying to get more information about where we'd gone. I kept my answers vague.

Mercy bolted awake when we stopped in front of her house, which turned out to be only a few blocks away.

"See you around!" I shouted as she trudged up to her front door. She merely yawned.

At my house, I was greeted by the full fury of my mother.

"Nathaniel James Clark," she declared from the doorway, her nostrils flaring. "Where the hell have you been?

Your uncle told me kids were going missing. You had me worried half to death."

"Mom," I said, and then I couldn't help myself. I stepped forward and gave her a big hug. I'd been so scared, and it was such a relief to be back, to be safe.

She grabbed my shoulders and held me out at arm's length.

"Are you okay?" she asked, her tone suddenly worried instead of angry.

"Yeah," I said. "And it's all fine now, we found the kid."

My mother frowned at me. "Well, I'm just glad you're all right."

She gave me another hug and then allowed me to escape to my room. I went straight to my computer and sent a long email to my friend Rudy at camp, telling him all about how *Voidjumper* was a lot closer to reality than we'd previously believed.

That night, I dreamed of falling. Over and over, through an endless nothingness.

The next morning at breakfast, I asked my mother if I could go to Krazyland again.

"You put up such a fuss about it just yesterday," she said. "Now you WANT to go?"

"Um, yeah. I had a change of heart." The truth was that I was desperate to talk to Mercy again. With distance, the strange events of yesterday had taken on a sort of dreamlike quality. I could remember how terrified I'd been, but the terror itself had faded. Now all I wanted was to know more about how it all worked.

"Well," said my mother, "I suppose I can drop you off on my way to work."

"I can just bike there."

My mother was even more surprised by this. Her son willingly engaging in outdoor physical activity? I saw her narrowing her eyes at me, no doubt trying to determine if I was a changeling.

"All right," she said finally. "Just text me when you get there so I know you're okay."

I biked there so fast that I arrived early, well before Krazyland opened. Uncle Steven and Jake had only just arrived. My uncle seemed surprised to see me, but I told him I'd come to look for my lost phone—I also had him text my mom to tell her I had arrived safe.

I followed Uncle Steven inside, past the front desk and the restrooms, past the shoe cubby and the birthday room, into the heart of the beast.

Immediately, I could feel it. Something was wrong. Something was very wrong. It felt like all the air had been sucked right out of the room, like the whole place was holding its breath.

Even Uncle Steven seemed to notice it. He frowned, scanning the cavernous room full of twisting plastic tubes, trampolines, and games.

I followed as he wove his way past the Skee-Ball lanes,

past the spider-stomping game, past the corner with Big Bertha in it. I steeled my nerves and gave her a sideways glance.

But she was just the same as she'd always been before. A creepy arcade game, caged safely in a big metal box with plexiglass sides.

I stopped briefly at the prize counter to poke the inflatable bear toy sitting behind the counter. I felt reassured when it didn't move.

Up ahead, Uncle Steven had stopped. I knew before looking what he had stopped in front of. It was the giant pit of plastic balls, the one Mercy and I had fallen through. Uncle Steven was standing just outside the mesh enclosure, staring in.

I approached cautiously, my sense of unease growing with every step. I had no idea what I'd see when I got close enough.

But when I got there, I saw nothing. There was nothing to see. The pit was empty. The bare concrete floor showed through the uncovered mesh suspended across the bottom of the pit.

"We've been robbed," said Uncle Steven.

THE BUTT OF
THE WATER

I squinted at the empty pit. It hadn't been like this when we left yesterday. Moving closer, I spotted something—or sort of something. A vague scintillation of the air, a sort of shimmery blur, only visible if I moved my head back and forth. I was pretty sure I knew what I was looking at: a hole in reality.

It had not closed up like Mercy said it would. Instead, it had gotten worse.

Uncle Steven sent Jake into the stockroom to fetch some boxes of extra plastic balls.

"The levels tend to drop gradually over time," Uncle Steven explained, as he helped Jake dump the boxes into the pit. "It's always been like that. Since I first got the place. Maybe the kids smuggle them out in their shirts. I don't know."

It was all I could do not to say *Or maybe that pit is a*

gateway between this world and a totally freaky one, but I kept my mouth shut.

"It's never been this bad, though," said Uncle Steven.

I kept glancing over at the prize counter to see if Mercy had shown up yet. Maybe she'd be able to explain this.

When Uncle Steven and Jake finished emptying the boxes, the pit was barely half full.

"You dumped them all in there?" Uncle Steven asked. Jake confirmed that he had.

"Weird," he said. "That should have been more than enough."

Jake was flattening out the cardboard boxes. There were dozens of them. It should have been way more than enough.

"Maybe you should just shut it down for the day," I suggested.

To my relief, Uncle Steven agreed that was probably for the best. He taped a flattened cardboard box over each tunnel that led to the pit and another over the main entrance, with *Closed for maintenance* written on them in Sharpie.

Mercy still hadn't shown up by the time Krazyland opened. I tracked down Jake at the front desk and asked if he knew where she was.

He shrugged. "She's late all the time. Dad should really fire her and hire somebody better. Our grandpa is dead, too, and nobody gives us special treatment."

He was referring to the father of Uncle Steven and my mother, who had passed away before I was born. Our grandma remarried, though, and Pops, as we called her husband, was a pretty cool dude, so that was all right.

"Did you ever meet him?" I asked. "Mercy's grandfather I mean."

"Nope."

"Do you know how he died?"

"You're such a creepy little weirdo. How should I know? Leave me alone and go read the plaque or something." He waved vaguely at the wall behind him and then plastered on a smile as some customers arrived.

There was a plaque, it turned it out, though I had never noticed it before. It was silver, engraved with the words:

> IN MEMORY OF GERALD RIVERBOTTOM,
> CHERISHED FATHER AND GRANDFATHER,
> WHO HAD A VISION FOR A LAND OF FUN.

Below that were dates of birth and death, which confirmed what Mercy had told me. He'd died about two years ago. Above the inscription was a rough likeness in profile that did indeed look very much like the man I'd seen being devoured by Bertha the day before.

So what did that mean? I couldn't be sure. All I knew was I really needed to talk to Mercy.

And also that her last name was Riverbottom. No wonder she was so grumpy all the time!

WHOOPS

I decided to appoint myself guardian of the ball pit. I posted up in front of the foam stairs, arms crossed, expression severe, intent on preventing any children from bypassing the flimsy cardboard barrier and flinging themselves into the unknown.

The back of my neck prickled as I sat there. Was that the feel of reality leaking? Of nothingness reaching out to grope at the world and steal its shape?

Jake wandered over with a mop after I'd been sitting there for a while. I thought he was going to bug me, but instead he stared past me at the pit.

"What happened?" he asked.

"Huh?" I spun around. The balls he'd dumped in there this morning had practically all disappeared. About six or seven lolled around sadly at the bottom of the mesh, but that was it.

"Maybe there's a hole or something," he said. He

propped his mop against the side of the pit and moved toward the stairs.

"No!" I shouted immediately.

"What's your problem?" Jake scowled at me. "Did you take them?"

"Uh, no."

Jake rolled his eyes, tried to walk past me. I jumped to my feet and shifted sideways to block his path.

"Seriously," he said, "shove over, freak."

I thought fast. "Some kid puked! You don't want to go in there."

Jake paused, shot me a deeply suspicious look. "Now I know you're hiding something."

"How? I mean no, I'm not."

"You'd love nothing more than to see me step right into a pile of vomit," he shot back. "You have it out for me."

That was ridiculous. He was the one who had it out for me.

Before I could point that out, though, he pushed me roughly aside and jumped up the foam stairs.

I leapt after him and managed to grab hold of his ankle. He yelped as I pulled at his sock, and before I could do anything to stop it, we had both tumbled headlong into the pit.

BASICALLY JUST SOGGY CHIPS WITH NO TASTE

I didn't scream this time.

Jake did, though, which made me feel a little better as we both fell, hurtling first through the cloud of plastic balls, and then through emptiness. I caught a glimpse of him clawing at the air beneath me and then we both hit the trampoline.

Once he'd stopped bouncing, Jake immediately rounded on me.

"What did you do?" he demanded.

"I didn't do anything." I climbed shakily to my feet and glanced around. The place looked basically the same. The cloud of plastic balls overhead was slightly closer now, though not close enough that it would be easy to get back up to. Perhaps it had grown thanks to all the real balls falling through.

Jake gave a strangled cry. "What is that?"

My stomach dropped, a vivid memory of the giant

spider leaping to the forefront of my mind. But Jake was merely staring out at the emptiness beyond the trampolines—that greasy static our eyes couldn't interpret. It was like trying to focus on something too close to your face while simultaneously squinting at something too far away to see.

"Oh that," I said, adopting a tone of casual detachment. "It's nothing."

Somehow the presence of Jake and his obvious distress made me feel calmer. Perhaps it was because, unlike with Mercy, this time *I* was the one who knew more about the situation. I was in control. I was calm and collected. Cool as a cucumber. Although what exactly is so cool about a cucumber? I think they're kind of gross.

"It's horrible." Jake dropped to his knees, sending a ripple through the trampoline. He rubbed his eyes furiously. "How do I wake up?"

"You're not dreaming," I told him.

He slapped himself in the face. "Ow!" he cried.

"See," I said, trying not to laugh. "I told you. Chill out."

"Did I hit my head in the stupid ball pit? Do I have a concussion? Am I in a coma?"

"No," I said, "the ball pit is—"

He interrupted me. "You grabbed my foot—you knocked me over!"

"I didn't—"

He jumped to his feet, pointing an accusatory finger. "You were trying to kill me!"

"I was trying to save you!"

"Argh." He stalked off toward the other end of the trampoline, both hands tightened into fists.

Exasperated, I followed. If anyone should be angry, it was me. After all, it was his fault I was here, not the other way around. If he'd just listened to me in the first place, this whole thing could have been avoided.

Up ahead, Jake reached the end of the trampoline and stopped. As I drew closer, I saw that something was different. Instead of a long line of trampolines reaching into the distance, there was nothing else beyond this one.

And worse than that, there was a big half-moon chunk ripped out of the edge of this trampoline. Almost like a giant bite.

I knelt and touched the ragged edge of the trampoline fabric where it had been torn. Could spiders have done that? If so, they must be even bigger than the one I'd met before—not an appealing prospect.

Then again, who knew what other horrible creatures might lurk here. Krazyland had an off-brand Whac-A-Mole with plastic alligator heads. Suppose there were giant alligators that popped up unexpectedly? There was also this one extremely old arcade game that was a cheap knockoff of Jurassic Park. The graphics were so bad that the dinosaurs were just blocky lumps of pixels, but still. They might exist here as distorted reflections of reality.

"This can't be good," I said. I could feel my nervousness returning, did my best to suppress the slight tremble in my voice. Looking scared in front of Mercy had been embarrassing enough, but Jake would definitely mock me for it. "It wasn't like this last time."

Jake scowled down at me. "What do you mean last time?"

"I fell through here once before. That's why I was trying to keep you from going into the ball pit. It's like a portal to another dimension." I knew it was a bit more complicated than that, but Jake didn't seem to be in the mood for technicalities.

"This is the stupidest thing that ever happened to me," said Jake. He cupped his hands around his mouth and shouted into the void. "Hello! Anybody? Get me out of here!"

I poked him in the arm. My heart was beating faster now. "Be quiet."

"Why should I?"

"There's giant spiders here. They might hear you."

"I'm not afraid of spiders," he scoffed. "Only dumb babies are afraid of spiders."

"Uh, right," I said, nervously scanning the horizon. "I mean, same here. Spiders are great. Some of my best friends are spiders."

Jake wasn't paying any attention to me. "HELP!" he shouted. "I'm stuck here with my stupid cousin!"

I turned my own attention up to the cloud, tried to keep my thoughts calm and practical. We needed to get up there to escape. There were no flying animals handy— not that I'd trust them anyway.

Last time the reverse avalanche had allowed us to defy gravity. Surely the cloud up there was defying it, too. Plastic balls are heavier than gaseous water vapor. There was no reason they should be floating in the air.

Gravity in this place was apparently more of a suggestion than a law. If only I could convince myself that up was down and down was up, maybe I could bypass it.

Standing on my head seemed like a good start. I made an attempt, but toppled over immediately.

"What the heck are you doing?" Jake asked. "Have you lost your mind?"

I sat up with a sigh and did my best to explain my gravity theory and how it could help us get home. I could tell he was itching to call me an idiot, but sense prevailed long enough for him to listen.

"So I think it's just like a mind-over-matter thing," I finished up. "That's why I was trying to get upside down."

Jake considered. "What if I held your legs?"

I didn't relish the idea, but I couldn't think of anything better. A few uncomfortable moments later, Jake had me hoisted by the ankles.

I closed my eyes. *My head isn't pressing down on the trampoline,* I told myself, *the trampoline is pressing down on my head.* I repeated it over and over. I felt sure I was almost there, right on the edge of believing it.

Jake grunted and let go of my legs.

I fell, not up to the cloud, but back down to the trampoline.

"You're really heavy for someone so short," he said.

"Maybe you're just weak," I fired back, but immediately regretted it. I rolled away as Jake made a grab for me, most likely intent on grievous bodily harm. As I scrambled to my feet, I spotted something.

"Wait," I said, pointing. "Look."

There was a shape floating through the air out in the distance. I thought for a moment it might be the inflatable bear or lion coming to save us.

But then it moved closer and I realized how very wrong I was.

HIGH-ALTITUDE GYMNASTICS

One of the games back in Krazyland was called the Cyclone. It consisted of a clear plastic dome with a ring of multicolored lights beneath it. The lights flashed one by one in sequence, very fast. You were supposed to hit a button and make the lights stop at one specific point.

But I'd learned early on that the game was totally rigged. Uncle Steven had set it up so that it wasn't even possible to win most of the time, no matter how accurate you were.

An enormous version of that dome, true to its name, was now spinning through the air toward me and Jake. It resembled a flying saucer with all those blinking lights.

And sitting atop it was none other than Big Bertha.

Definitely not possible to win.

"Run," I said to Jake.

"Why?"

"She's dangerous."

Jake gave me a pitying look, then turned and walked *toward* the approaching cyclone.

I took my own advice and booked it in the opposite direction.

"Hey you!" I heard Jake shouting behind me. "Yeah you, on the spaceship. We need help."

"YOU," boomed the voice of Bertha. I stopped running and glanced back. The cyclone saucer was hovering just past the edge of the trampoline now. Bertha pointed an enormous finger at Jake. Was she even bigger than she had been last time? I thought so.

"You are real," she declared.

"Duh," said Jake. "I need a ride up to that dumb cloud-looking thing."

It was a bold move. Honestly, in that moment I admired my cousin. Was there any chance it would work? Bertha would certainly be capable of lifting us up to the cloud.

"Tell me a story," said Bertha.

"What?"

"Tell me a story about your world."

"No," said Jake. "This is stupid."

"A STORY," thundered Bertha so loud I felt the wind of her breath. I started backing up slowly, ready to turn and run again at any moment.

"You don't get to order me around," said Jake. "You're not even real. You're just a weird arcade game of a fat lady."

Whatever admiration I'd had for Jake's bravery plummeted to the ground and died a fiery death. He wasn't brave, he was just a bully. Don't insult the person you are trying to get to help you! Especially not if she's a literal giant who could crush you in the palm of one hand.

Jake had called me fat before, too, and, sure, it was accurate, but I knew he said it because he was trying to make me feel bad about myself. And it had worked.

Bertha frowned, her mouth like a canyon in the wide prairie of her face. She was bigger than last time for sure.

"Not real," she said. She sounded surprisingly sad, as though that was the part of Jake's diatribe that had insulted her. "Yes. But you will help me."

She reached out for Jake. He aimed a kick at her hand.

"Leave me alone," he said.

I'd like to say that I bravely ran forward to save him, but I did not. Was it because I sort of thought Jake was a jerk and he deserved what was coming to him? Was it because I was selfish? Was it because I was simply too scared to move?

I'm not sure. But the fact remains that I watched, frozen, as Bertha scooped up Jake. He got in a few more ill-advised insults and expletives before her fingers closed around him, muffling his voice. She glanced from her fist back to the trampoline, eyes searching.

That, finally, pushed me into motion. Small as I was compared to her, there was nowhere to hide on a giant trampoline. She would spot me for sure.

I ran toward the center, thinking she couldn't reach me there, but that was foolish. She was on a flying machine—she could get anywhere. When I glanced over my shoulder, I saw that the cyclone had risen into the air above the trampoline. It floated inexorably forward.

I stopped running just short of the opposite end of the trampoline. It was time to really put my theory to the test. I had just one chance.

I knelt at the edge of the trampoline, draped myself over the side so that my head and arms dangled into nothingness. I closed my eyes.

I visualized as clearly as I could what I intended, silently told gravity to take a hike.

Then I kicked my legs up off the trampoline and swung my torso forward. If it didn't work, I would simply fall. For a terrifying moment there was nothing holding me, my legs flailing. A powerful wave of dizziness overcame me. I grasped desperately out, fingers scrabbling at the air.

My hand met fabric. I opened my eyes.

I could barely believe it. It had worked. I had flipped onto the underside of the trampoline, and "gravity" had flipped, too. My legs hung off the edge, dangling down now toward the ball cloud.

I saw Bertha floating upside down below me. Her left fist was still closed tight. I thought I heard a muffled shout from within, but I might have imagined it.

I let go.

WAKE-UP CALL

B ack in the real world, I hauled myself out of the pit, which was now completely empty, and ran down the steps. My pulse pounded in my ears, almost as loud as Bertha's voice. I'd only barely gotten away.

I found Uncle Steven in the kitchen area, furiously microwaving a slice of pizza and grumbling under his breath.

"Is Mercy here yet?" I gasped, still slightly breathless from my fall through the world.

"Isn't she?" He looked up, brow creased. "I suppose I haven't seen her. Does that mean the prize counter is unattended?"

I hurriedly cut him off before he could send me to go get Jake or something. "You should call her and tell her to come in. Maybe she overslept."

The microwave dinged. Uncle Steven removed the paper plate of gluey cheese and mushy dough that just barely qualified as pizza and slid it over to the kid waiting at the order window.

"Excuse me," said a man waiting behind the kid. "There's no one at the front desk."

Uncle Steven made a noise of exasperation. "One second, sir. I can help you." He pulled his phone from his pocket and shoved it into my hands. "Here, you call her."

He pushed past me out of the kitchen, shouting for Jake, who I knew very well would not respond.

I was briefly tempted to log in to my email and check to see if Rudy had responded to my message from the night before. But I resisted and scrolled through Uncle Steven's contacts instead.

There was no listing for Mercy, but I remembered the plaque and scrolled until I found a listing with same last name—Olive Riverbottom.

I dialed.

A girl's voice answered. "Hello?"

"Mercy?" I asked.

"No. Taxi."

"What?"

"I'm Taxi. Mercy is my sister."

"Oh. Well can I speak to her?"

"She's asleep."

Somehow, I was not surprised. "Okay, can you wake her up?"

"She'll be mad at me if I do."

"But she needs to come to work—it's kind of an emergency."

"Sorry," said Taxi, and she abruptly ended the call.

My finger hovered over the icon to call back, but this truly was an emergency. Reality was clearly leaking worse than ever and Jake was gone. If Taxi didn't want to bother her sister, I'd have to do it myself.

I snuck out. Not that Uncle Steven was in any position to pay attention to what I was doing, burdened as he was with running the entire place by himself.

Luckily, it was a super-short bike ride to Mercy's house. The day before, from the car, her house had looked like a nice little Cape Cod, with light gray siding and a garden in front. When I got close, however, it became apparent that the siding, which was cracked and bent in places, had originally been white. It just looked gray because of all the built-up dirt. There were shingles falling off the roof and the gutters were filled with dead leaves. The garden out front was composed entirely of weeds.

I knocked. Flakes of paint chipped off where my fist hit the wood.

After a minute or so the door swung open and I was faced with a girl who looked about my age, or maybe a year or two younger—Taxi, presumably.

"Hi," I said. "I'm Nathan, from Krazyland. We just spoke on the phone."

She looked me up and down, with a hint of judgment. She resembled Mercy very much in that moment.

"Yeah, she mentioned you. The boss's annoying nephew."

I decided to ignore that and forge ahead. "I really need to talk to Mercy."

Taxi shrugged. "Fine. Come on in."

The inside of the house was much like the outside. I nearly tripped over a pile of books on the way in. The wallpaper was peeling off the wall in long strips. There was a flowerpot tipped over in the corner of the entryway alcove, spilling dirt and dead petunias across the scratched wood floor.

"She's upstairs," said Taxi, heading into the living room, where the TV was on. "She sleeps a lot. It's because of her allergies. I have them, too, but not as bad."

Taxi plopped down cross-legged on the floor rather than the ratty-looking sofa, and returned to watching cartoons. For a moment I wished fervently that I could be at home, carefree, watching television.

And I realized that if I really wanted to, I could. I could get back on my bike and race all the way back to my house. Could run up to my room, lock the door, play *Voidjumper*. Let all this be someone else's problem.

Part of me wanted that, but I decided I was going to be brave. I was going to do this even though it scared me.

I was going to save my bully of a cousin. And possibly the whole world. Possibly all of reality.

THE OTHER ONE

In the first room I checked upstairs, a figure was asleep in a bed, facing away from me. I crept in, but when I got around to the other side of the bed, I saw the sleeping figure wasn't Mercy at all. It was an adult lady—her mother, I assumed. Sleeping a lot must be a family trait.

I tiptoed backward out of the room, terrified the whole time that the woman would wake up and freak out.

The next room I checked had two twin beds, one of them occupied.

"Mercy?" I whispered. She was wrapped up in the blanket burrito-style, her hair half over her face. I snuck closer. She snored gently and rolled over. Definitely her.

It felt a bit rude, but there was no time to waste. I reached out, tentatively, and poked her shoulder.

She bolted upright instantly. Her eyes fell upon me, accusing.

"What are you doing here?" she said.

"Sorry," I said, backing up instinctively in case she tried to brain me with a pillow. "You didn't show up to work."

She grabbed her phone from the bedside table and swore when she saw the time.

"All right," she said. "I'm up now. You can run back and tell Mr. Clark I'll be there soon."

"My uncle didn't send me. I . . . I need your help. Something is wrong with the, uh . . ." Here in the light of day it felt absurd to say *the other world,* even though I'd just been there. "With the ball pit."

She sighed and rubbed her eyes. "Okay, wait downstairs. I'll be there in a moment."

I trudged back down the stairs. Taxi was focused on the television and didn't even turn around. I stood awkwardly in the hallway until Mercy came down, dressed in her uniform now.

She ushered me into the kitchen so we could talk away from Taxi. The room was small and dingy, the wood of the cabinets warped by water damage and the stove missing three of its four burners. One of the overhead cabinets had fallen off the wall and was propped up in the corner.

"So, what's going on?" Mercy asked, leaning against the counter, inches away from a precarious stack of mismatched dishes.

"The rip in reality is still there," I told her.

She frowned. "Are you sure? Bringing all the real people out of Nowhere should have fixed it."

"I'm sure. I went to Krazyland this morning because I wanted to ask you more about what happened yesterday, but when I got there, all the balls in the big ball pit were gone. And then I fell through again!"

"What? How?"

I gave her a quick recap of the dramatic events that had so recently transpired.

"Ugh," she said, when I finished. "I should have stayed asleep."

"Do you know why this is happening? Is it because of the real stuff that fell in there? Like that bouncy ball you found?" I was pretty sure my phone was in there, too. And probably tons of the ball-pit balls.

"I don't think so," said Mercy. "I mean, most of what I know is just what my mother told me when I was younger. According to her, if you break through to Nowhere, the best thing to do is get back out quickly. It's also best to leave nothing behind, like camping. If you leave inanimate objects in there, they'll continue to exist and generate a small field of reality around themselves, but everything will remain static and unchanging."

"Oh dang," I exclaimed. "That's just like *Voidjumper!*"

In the game there was a specific item—an anchor—that you had to place in any new world you visited if you wanted to be able to visit it again. Otherwise, the code for that world would just delete itself when you left.

"What?" said Mercy.

"It's a game," I said. "A video game."

"Right, well, the way my mother told it, it's only the presence of real people that allows Nowhere to siphon off reality. It shouldn't have been able to get any worse after we left. Every time I leave the other—"

She cut herself off abruptly.

"The other what?" I asked.

She sighed, pushed away from the counter. "I guess there's something I should show you."

THE TRUE FATE OF MISSING SOCKS

I followed Mercy down a narrow staircase, which led to a dimly lit basement. She pointed to the dryer, which sat against the wall with its door hanging open.

"Go in there," she told me.

"What? Is this a prank? No."

A few years back, Jake had managed to trick me into the garden shed by claiming he'd seen a frog in there, only to shut the door and lock me in. It was probably only ten minutes or so before someone heard me shouting and let me out, but it had felt like much longer.

"Don't worry," Mercy said, "it's been broken for years. When I was younger, I would sit in here and pretend it was a deep-sea submarine or the escape pod of a starship. Somewhere vast and dark and very far away."

"Um, cool?"

"Go on," said Mercy. She nudged me in the shoulder. Resigned, I crawled into the dryer. It wasn't very comfortable. I had to sit hunched over with my knees drawn all the way up to my chest.

"Notice anything weird?" Mercy asked.

"Well, I'm in a dryer. That's pretty weird."

She snorted. "Anything else?"

I had an idea of the sort of things I was supposed to be noticing: a strange noise or a tingling up the back of my neck. I closed my eyes, but I felt nothing out of the ordinary, heard nothing. I even tried sniffing the air, but everything smelled normal, too.

"No." I felt a bit sheepish, as though I'd failed a test

"Okay, now hit the back wall of the dryer."

I did as I was told. There was a resounding metallic sound that rang in my ears in the closed space. My palm stung a bit. Nothing else happened.

"What was the point of that?" I asked.

"I just wanted to show you that nothing would happen."

"So this *was* a prank!"

Mercy laughed. "Maybe a little. Now get out of there."

Relieved that I hadn't been spun out into interdimensional oblivion, I extracted myself from the dryer. Mercy took my place. She was even more scrunched up than I had been in the small space. She closed her eyes.

"What are you doing?" I asked.

Mercy held up a shushing finger. "Now I have to start again."

"Start what?"

"If there's not already a rip in reality," she said, eyes still closed, "breaking through to Nowhere takes conscious effort. You have to make your mind go totally blank and maintain that for several minutes. Most people can't do it at all, but my family has a knack for it. Now be quiet so I can focus."

I shifted from foot to foot, impatient. What if somebody else fell into the pit while we were messing about down here?

Mercy remained silent and still for a long time. Long enough that I was genuinely convinced she'd fallen asleep. But then, finally, she opened her eyes and said, "Okay. That did it."

She shifted herself around in the dryer and crawled forward—but not out into the basement. No, she turned away from me and crawled, somehow, deeper into the dryer, disappearing into darkness.

"Mercy!" I shouted, but she was gone from view.

What choice did I have? I followed.

A LEAK IN THE BASEMENT

crawled into the dryer. I crawled out of the dryer.

I hadn't turned around, though. I'd gone straight. I was sure of it. Mercy was standing in the middle of the basement, waiting for me.

"We're nowhere," I said.

She nodded. "A different part of it. Come see."

We walked back up the stairs to the kitchen. Or at least, to a kitchen.

The layout was the same. The counters and the stove were in the same place they had been. The window over the sink was still over the sink. The walls were covered in the same flowery wallpaper. The floor was covered in the same checked linoleum.

But there were no cracks in the linoleum. The wallpaper wasn't faded or peeling. The stove wasn't coated in a layer of rust as thick as birthday-cake icing. The wood of the cabinets was unwarped.

I wandered into the living room. Once again, the room looked the same as I remembered, just nicer. I noticed a small porcelain cat sitting in the center of the coffee table.

"That's the only real thing here," Mercy said, gesturing at the cat. "I brought it through. It keeps this version of the house stable, but the hole in my basement still seals itself up each time I leave. You saw how I had to concentrate to get back through. I wouldn't be able to just fall in by accident. Nobody would."

"It all looks so normal," I said, turning to Mercy. "It's nothing like the place on the other side of the ball pit."

"Try the door," she said, pointing.

I opened the front door—

And immediately slammed it shut again.

"Never mind," I said.

Just beyond the front door had been nothing. The front steps led not to a lawn, but to that same roiling, sizzling visual white noise that had filled the horizon in the other Nowhere. There was no sidewalk, no street. The world began and ended with this house.

"You're right, though," admitted Mercy. "This place is much smaller and less weird than the part of Nowhere we fell into at Krazyland, probably because I'm very careful never to stay here long. My mother told me that as soon as a real person enters Nowhere, it can feed off their perceptions to grow and change, but as soon as they leave, it can't. Nowhere has no imagination. It needs people."

"Things had definitely changed there." I told Mercy about the trampoline with the bite taken out, about how much bigger Bertha had gotten.

"We must not have gotten all the real people out, after all," said Mercy. "It's the only explanation."

I coughed. "Um, about that. Remember I said I saw a guy who looked like your grandfather?"

Mercy scowled, but I forged ahead.

"What if he was real," I said, "and that's why the hole wasn't fixed?"

"He's dead, though. I went to his funeral."

"Was it an open casket?"

Mercy fixed me with a look of utter disbelief. I realized, a moment too late, that this had been a very weird and possibly rude question.

"I'm sorry," I said. "It just—it would explain things, wouldn't it?"

"I guess." Mercy turned away, so I couldn't see her expression.

I felt guilty for upsetting her, but somehow, I couldn't quite let it go. Could her grandfather have faked his death? I lowered my voice, did my best to ask the next part gently. "Can I . . . can I ask how he died?"

She didn't answer for a moment. When she finally spoke, her voice was a bit strained.

"Mom said it was probably a stroke. I . . . I think a neighbor stopped by or something and found him unconscious. His heart had stopped. It was too late to save him."

"Oh," I said. I was about to apologize again, when Mercy whipped around suddenly to face me, her eyes wide. She didn't look angry or sad anymore, but shocked. "Wait. That's how he did it."

"Did what?"

"None of us were there," she said, voice rising with something that sounded suspiciously like excitement. "The neighbor called 911. The EMTs couldn't resuscitate him. He wasn't breathing. He didn't have a heartbeat!"

"Um." I was very lost. "What?"

"You were right," she said. "The one who died—it wasn't him."

CHUNK ERROR

Mercy was pacing around the small living room. She picked up the porcelain cat, set it back down.

"So you're saying he did fake his own death?" I asked.

"I think so. It seems so obvious now, but we had no reason to suspect anything at the time." She shook her head. "This would mean the hole in reality has been there for even longer than I realized. It was bad enough that John had been there for two months, but two years? That's really dangerous."

"It is?" I felt a flush of guilt for not trying harder to save Jake.

Mercy nodded. "The longer you stay, the worse it is. A few generations back, a great-great-great aunt of mine broke through and stayed so long that the barrier between our world and Nowhere destabilized entirely. Her whole house fell through. It left a seventy-five-foot-deep sinkhole. The hole is still there—my mother took me to see it once. There's a row of normal houses and then just a gaping chasm in the middle. It looks like a glitch—like someone accidentally deleted a chunk of the earth."

"Uh-oh." I thought of the empty ball pit—was the balls' falling through just a precursor to the entirety of Krazyland falling right out of the world?

"Maybe if any of us had been there when he was found, we would have figured it out."

I frowned. "I still don't quite understand—how did your grandfather convince everyone he was dead?"

"I'll show you," said Mercy. She turned and shouted up the stairs. "Mother!"

A woman appeared at the top of the steps. She descended, smiling. I was relieved for a moment, thinking she had come to help us with the Krazyland problem, but then I remembered the woman I'd seen sleeping in the bed earlier. If this was Mercy's mother, then who had that been?

"Hello, dear," the woman said.

"Mother," said Mercy, "this is Nathan. Nathan, this is Mother."

"Um, hello." I looked back and forth between the two of them. Mercy's mother was smiling blankly at me. She wasn't blinking.

I remembered what Mercy had told me the day before: Nowhere could copy anything from the real world, including people. But it got the details wrong.

"Do you understand now?" Mercy asked.

"Uh, no?"

Mercy sighed. Instead of even trying to explain, she grabbed her mother—her *fake* mother, I was pretty sure—by the hand and marched into the kitchen. I hurried after them as they headed down the basement stairs.

When I reached the basement, Mercy was leading her mother over to the dryer. I ran forward and blocked their path.

"Hold on just a second," I said. "Stop. What are you doing?"

"See," she said, "this is how he did it."

Before I could protest further, Mercy skirted around me and climbed into the dryer. The fake mother dutifully followed and Mercy pulled her through to the other side.

AN UNUSUALLY LONG NAP

Crawling back through to the real world was like walking out of a dark movie theater into the bright afternoon sun.

Except it wasn't the light that was brighter, exactly, but everything else. The smells were brighter. The sounds were brighter. The air felt brighter against my skin.

I blinked at the fake mother, who was standing next to Mercy beside the dryer, still smiling, of course.

"Oh," I said. I'd had no idea that fake people from Nowhere could cross over into our world. A terrible thought struck me. "Wait a second. If she can come out of Nowhere, does that mean other things could, too?"

"Sure," said Mercy. "Though if you're thinking of the giant spider"—I flinched as she said it. I had very much been thinking of the giant spider—"I suspect it would have trouble moving around out here, faced with the actual laws of physics."

Somehow that was no less awful of an image.

Mercy must have seen my look of horror, because she went on. "Don't worry, though, they aren't going to just crawl out on their own. Someone real needs to pull them through."

I could see it now: Jake returning triumphant and vengeful, an army of arachnids behind him, ready to hunt to me down.

"Your grandfather," I said, with sudden realization. "You think he brought out a fake copy of himself?"

Mercy nodded. "When the neighbor found him, he wasn't breathing and he had no pulse—well, fake people never do in my experience. That's just too complicated to copy."

I looked closer at the fake mother. Indeed, she didn't seem to be breathing. No doubt she didn't have to.

"Come on," said Mercy, heading up the stairs to the kitchen. The fake mother trailed after her.

"Don't we need to put her back?" I asked, running after them.

"We have to go find my grandfather," said Mercy, her tone matter-of-fact. "That won't be easy. If we're gone for a long time or if anything happens to me . . ." She trailed off, and I swallowed down a spike of fear at the implication. This would be dangerous.

"Well," Mercy finished, "I don't want to leave Taxi on her own too long."

When we got to the kitchen, she grabbed a loaf of

bread and jars of peanut butter and jelly from the fridge and set them on the counter.

"Okay," she said to the fake mother. "I'm going out for a while. Make sure Taxi eats at some point, okay?"

"Yes, dear," said the fake mother.

"Why didn't you just go get your real mother?" I asked as we left. "She's upstairs, isn't she?"

Mercy closed the front door behind us and gave me a long look. She seemed to be considering something.

Finally, she turned away and said, "My mom hasn't woken up for two years."

"What?" I followed Mercy down the street toward Krazyland. "Shouldn't she be in a hospital?"

"They wouldn't be able to help." She waved a dismissive hand. "It's just our allergies."

That sounded like a lot more than just allergies. "Are you sure?"

Mercy shrugged. "She used to be like me. But when my granddad died—it was super sudden. He hadn't even been sick or anything." She was silent for a moment, probably thinking about what we now suspected: that her grandfather's death had been a ruse. "Well, anyway, my mom took it really hard. She started sleeping more and more until eventually she was just asleep all the time."

"So it's like a coma?"

"Not exactly. She sleepwalks. Sleep-eats and stuff. But she's not awake."

"What about your dad?" I asked, and then regretted it when I saw a flash of annoyance cross Mercy's face.

"He's not around," she said.

"Oh dang," I said. "Sorry."

"It's fine," said Mercy, but in that way that my parents sometimes say it's fine when what they actually mean is *it's really terrible but we feel the need to pretend it isn't.* "I already knew the dryer was a thin place, so one day when there were parent-teacher conferences at Taxi's school and I couldn't get my mom to wake up, I broke through and brought out a fake version of her. She can't stay out too long or she kind of just ... disintegrates and vanishes. Found that out the hard way."

She glanced over at me. "You know, you're the first person I've ever told all this. Or any of it, really."

I was startled. Mercy was giving me a funny look. Not annoyed like usual. She'd been almost maddeningly chill the day before, when we were facing down giants and giant spiders in Nowhere, but now she looked nervous.

"Cool," I said. "I mean, that all sounds like a lot. But I'm glad you told me."

Mercy gave me a small smile before she turned away, so quick I nearly missed it.

I thought of my friend Rudy, how great it had been to finally have someone I could talk to about all the stuff that interested me without getting weird looks.

Maybe Rudy wasn't my only friend anymore.

WHO'S ON FIRST

Back at Krazyland, Mercy and I surveyed the empty ball pit.

"You were right," she said. She moved closer and held a hand over the pit. "It's leaking even worse than before. I can feel it. If my grandfather is in there, we need to get him out as soon as possible."

"Can people die in Nowhere?" I asked. I was thinking about *Voidjumper*, where death just resets you back home.

I was also thinking about Jake. When I left him, he'd been clutched in Bertha's massive fist. Maybe he'd decided to cooperate and tell her some stories. But maybe she'd decided he wasn't worth the trouble. Maybe she'd gotten too hungry.

Bertha had eaten Mercy's grandfather without hesitation, after all. But he must still be alive, right? He had to be, or our quest was futile. Maybe she'd swallowed him whole. Maybe he'd crawled back up her throat.

The alternative was simply too terrible to imagine.

"I'm not sure," said Mercy, which was not the answer I was hoping for.

We were interrupted by Uncle Steven hustling past with an armful of paper napkins. "Oh thank goodness," he said when he spotted Mercy, "there you are. I need you to get to the prize counter pronto, there's a line."

He gestured, releasing a small flurry of napkins, and then continued speed-walking back to the kitchen.

"We have to tell him what's going on," I said, realizing it for myself as I spoke the words aloud.

Mercy frowned. "He wouldn't believe us."

"He's going to realize his son is gone sooner or later."

Mercy shrugged as if to say *Not my problem.*

"And when we go back in there, we'll disappear, too. Uncle Steven will call the police again and our parents—" I paused, reconsidered. "Well, *my* parents will freak out. And your fake mother might not be very good at speaking to the police. What if she disintegrates in front of them?"

Mercy seemed to waver. "I guess we should say *something*. We could pretend Jake got sick and left?"

"We should just tell him the truth."

Maybe if I'd been honest with Jake, he'd still be safe and sound in the real world, bullying me in comfort and not potentially dead from getting eaten by a giant.

"He won't believe—" Mercy started to say, but I was already running to the kitchen.

"Uncle Steven!" I shouted as I approached.

He glanced up briefly before returning to his deep-frying. "Have you seen Jake?" he asked me. "Sometimes I don't even know why I have employees. I'm clearly the only one who does any work around here."

"Well, look," I said. "I need to talk to you about that. You know that kid who went missing?"

"Of course."

"Well Jake is missing, too."

"What?" He turned and gave me his full attention for the first time, brow creased. "What do you mean? He was here this morning."

"Yeah, but he's gone now, and he went to the same place that kid did, and I know where that is."

"Is this some kind of joke?"

"No, it's just . . . I mean, it's hard to explain."

"Stop talking in riddles, Nathan. Where's my son?"

"Um," I faltered, my courage failing. I hadn't really thought about how awkward this next part would be. "Mercy knows, too. She can explain it better."

Mercy looked none too pleased when I returned to the ball pit with a fuming Uncle Steven in tow.

"What kind of game are you kids playing?" he demanded. "I'm trying to run a business here you know."

Mercy glared at me. "We aren't playing any game, sir."

"Do you know where my son is?"

She sighed. "Yes."

"Where?"

"Nowhere."

"Where?"

"I told you. Nowhere."

"I am not in the mood for jokes." Uncle Steven was getting red in the face, his patience clearly running out.

"I told you he wouldn't believe us," Mercy said to me.

"Uncle Steven," I said. "Jake is in trouble. He's gone somewhere dangerous. It's partially my fault and I'm really sorry about that, but he needs our help."

He frowned at me. He opened his mouth. Closed it.

"You're serious, aren't you," he said.

I nodded.

"Okay," he said. His voice had changed. He didn't sound mad anymore, but worried. "Tell me what to do."

ARISTOTLE WAS ALSO WRONG

Uncle Steven closed Krazyland early again. He claimed there was a problem with the electricity and kicked everyone out with apologies and gift certificates for a free visit in the future. He also left a message for my mother and told her I'd be hanging out with him and Jake for the rest of the day.

Now the front door was locked, and the place was empty except for the three of us.

"I still don't understand," Uncle Steven said as we walked back toward the ball pit. He was eating some mozzarella sticks he'd microwaved for himself. He'd told me junk food calmed his nerves, but he didn't look calm. He looked tense. And greasy.

"There are weak spots in this world," Mercy said. "Like thin ice on a frozen pond. You've probably walked right over them dozens of times and not even noticed. Most people don't. But just like with real ice, if it cracks, you can fall through to the other side."

I looked over at Uncle Steven. His brow was creased, but he wasn't accusing us of playing a prank anymore.

"And the other side," he said. "That's another world?"

"Yeah," I said.

"No," said Mercy.

"Yes and no?" I suggested.

"Strictly speaking, it's not a world," said Mercy. "It's absolute nothingness. Aristotle believed that a perfect vacuum—a space completely empty of everything—could not exist. Nobody has ever created a perfect vacuum, maybe, but they do exist. On the other side of reality."

"So that's where Jake is?" asked Uncle Steven.

Mercy nodded.

"And it's under this building?"

"No," she said. "It's Nowhere. But we can get there from here. Hold on a moment."

We were just passing the prize counter. Mercy vaulted over the counter and grabbed the inflatable bear from the display.

"What's that for?" asked Uncle Steven.

"We might need transportation."

Uncle Steven shot me a questioning look. I just shrugged. He'd find out soon enough.

When we reached the pit, we stood in silence for a moment, contemplating the abyss. Except it didn't look like an abyss. It looked like some black netting suspended across a foam mat and supported by foam-covered poles.

"What happens when you jump?" asked Uncle Steven.

"You fall," I said.

"Well, yes," said Uncle Steven, "I could have guessed that part."

"You fall," said Mercy, "and then you land on a big trampoline."

"Doesn't sound too bad," said Uncle Steven.

"It isn't," said Mercy.

"She's lying," I interjected. "It's awful. There's a giant spider and the sky is completely empty and it's totally creepy."

Mercy lifted the inflatable bear over her head and heaved it into the middle of the pit. There was a sort of *POP* but without sound. Like if the air were a soap bubble stuck with a pin. The bear vanished.

Uncle Steven stared at the place where it had just been.

"Are you sure it's safe?" he asked.

"No," said Mercy. "It's definitely not."

THE MARIANA TRENCH
BUT MORE SO

W e jumped and, of course, we fell. This was my third time in two days, and, I've got to tell you, it was taking its toll. I was sore all over, and polka-dotted with tiny purplish bruises. Hollow plastic balls may seem harmless, but when you are hurtling through an ocean of them, believe me, they hurt.

I hit the trampoline and bounced around until my momentum finally slowed. Mercy helped me to my feet.

Uncle Steven was sprawled nearby, blinking rapidly. The bear Mercy had thrown through earlier padded over and sniffed at him.

Uncle Steven yipped and curled into a tight ball, his arms wrapped protectively around his head, though the bear was no bigger than a golden retriever.

I wanted to laugh, but I also remembered how scared I had been of the other bear. This one was much smaller— it hadn't changed shape or size when it fell through, though it had miraculously gained the power of loco-motion.

I supposed that was a bit like the gravity here. This place didn't know the rules, so it just extrapolated the best it could. The plastic bear *looked* like a living being, after all.

Mercy snapped her fingers. "Here, boy."

The bear left Uncle Steven alone and trotted obedi-ently over.

I knelt beside my uncle and gave him an awkward pat on the shoulder. "Um, hey, Uncle Steven? You okay?"

He whimpered.

"I guess I should have brought more than one," said Mercy, regarding the small bear. "Well, you and I can go, Nathan, and find the other animals and then come back for Mr. Clark."

My legs betrayed me. I sat down abruptly. The mem-ory of the moment when the giraffe popped midair felt fresh and vivid. I could still feel that lurch in my stomach when I'd dropped.

I'd hoped I could stay calmer this time around, now that I knew more or less what was happening, but I felt my pulse quicken, my breathing go shallow.

"Maybe I should, um, just stay here," I said.

Mercy squinted at me. "Oh, you're scared, aren't you?"

I opened my mouth to lie, to say *Of course not, I just thought I should keep an eye on my dear uncle.*

But it was no use. I *was* scared. I was even getting light-headed. It must have been clear from my face.

"Yeah," I said. My voice came out small. I hunched my shoulders, ready for Mercy to mock me.

"It'll be okay," she said, in what had to be the least harsh tone I'd ever heard her use. She almost sounded like she meant it. "I'll run recon, see about *you-know-who*, and then come back for you two."

She swung a leg over the bear, gave it a pat on the rump, and flew away into the empty sky, leaving me alone with my uncle on a trampoline in the middle of Nowhere. I wasn't sure if by *you-know-who* she meant Bertha, Jake, or her grandfather. We hadn't told Uncle Steven that a man he believed to be dead might in fact be alive and actively causing chaos.

Uncle Steven, for his part, remained tightly curled into a fetal position, face buried in his arms.

Perhaps it was harder for adults to adjust. John had seemed all right, but he'd had a while to get used to it, and he'd only been able to make sense of it by deciding he was dead.

I nudged Uncle Steven in the shoulder several times, then I bounced up and down on the trampoline to see if I could jiggle him out of his frozen state. Finally, I gave up and simply sat beside him in silence, waiting.

My panic had abated, and I was starting to feel guilty about not going with Mercy. What if she needed help?

Just sitting here, not knowing whether she was okay, was almost worse. I felt tense and restless.

I realized, with a sudden jolt, that I'd only told her about seeing her grandfather—I never told her that I'd seen Bertha eat him. I guess I hadn't wanted to upset her, and then I'd just forgotten, but that was a problem. We needed to find him and get him out of here, but how could we if he was currently being digested?

Beside me, Uncle Steven finally sat up and looked cautiously around.

"What is this place?" he asked, his voice a strained whisper.

"Nowhere," I said, "just like Mercy told you." But because I am kinder than Mercy, I added, "It's sort of like another dimension. Or maybe just a part of the normal dimension most people have never seen before."

I remembered my third-grade science teacher telling us that nearly two-thirds of the earth's surface was unexplored. Most of that was the ocean, especially the super-deep parts. No one had ever been to most of those parts. So maybe I'd think of Nowhere as just another ocean, except every part of it was the deepest part.

"Where's Jake?" my uncle asked.

"Not sure. But don't worry, we'll find him." I hoped that was true.

"That boy is always getting himself into trouble." Uncle Steven shook his head and seemed to dismiss his fear, but then his attention turned to something behind me. His eyes went wide.

I was overcome with a terrible sense of déjà vu.

"Remember how you mentioned something earlier about a giant spider?" he said.

I nodded, hoping against hope that the next thing out of his mouth would be something along the lines of: *Well, not to worry because there definitely isn't one behind you, ha ha, not even a little bit.*

"I thought you were joking at the time," Uncle Steven said, eyes still glued to some point past my left shoulder.

"And now?" I asked.

"Now I know you weren't."

TRIALS AND STRIDULATIONS

I turned, very slowly.

The spider was standing about twenty feet away from us, facing the other way. It was wearing green sneakers now, with yellow laces. Or perhaps this was a different spider.

"Maybe if we just stay really still, it won't see us," I said quietly.

"I can't stand spiders," muttered Uncle Steven from behind me. "Absolutely can't abide them. Never could. Ever since I was a kid."

The spider swiveled itself around and spotted us. I could only hope that if we didn't run, it wouldn't chase us.

"One summer," Uncle Steven went on, a note of hysteria creeping into his voice, "my parents shipped me off to camp. There was a whole nest of the things in our cabin. Cabin number five. I'll never forget it. They'd run across our faces at night. Worst summer of my life. I had to sleep with the sheets pulled up over my head. Nearly suffocated."

I sent some psychic sympathy to poor Rudy. Hopefully, his summer was going better than Uncle Steven's. Or mine, for that matter.

The spider took a step in our direction. Or rather, eight very small steps in our direction.

I thought again about what Mercy had said, how this place needed real people in order to exist, how it fed off their perceptions to shape itself.

What if I changed my perceptions? Perhaps a giant spider was only monstrous if I treated it like a monster.

"I'm not scared of you!" I shouted. It wasn't true, of course, but it was worth a try.

Uncle Steven tugged on my sleeve. "You don't want it coming over here, do you?"

"It's not real," I whispered, glancing back at him, "I think maybe we can talk it into being on our side."

Uncle Steven's expression suggested he didn't particularly want a giant spider on his side.

"You're totally harmless," I shouted at the spider. "You're about as threatening as a puppy in a pile of bubble wrap."

It seemed like it might be working. The spider hadn't come any closer.

"Yeah," added Uncle Steven, "I've washed worse than you down the drain of my bathtub, no sweat!"

Which was a mistake. The spider scuttled toward us, picking up speed as it went.

"Oh hell," said Uncle Steven. The trampoline jiggled under my feet as he turned and fled.

"He didn't mean it!" I shouted at the advancing behemoth. "Spiders are awesome! We would never harm a hair on their adorable cephalothoraxes. Please don't squish me!"

But it was too late. With a few quick bounds the spider reached me, and in one quick motion it had knocked me down and planted the foremost of its right legs firmly in the middle of my chest.

"Oof," I said.

Maybe some of what I'd shouted had made an impression, though, because the spider didn't press down. It just kept one massive foot resting, almost gently, on my chest, like a circus elephant doing a trick.

With the toe of its sneaker about three inches from my face, it occurred to me to wonder how exactly the spider was able to tie its shoes.

"Hey," I said, summoning every last shred of my tattered courage, "I realize that you've got, like, a personal mission to avenge the crimes committed against all spider-kind by the soles of shoes or something and I am one hundred percent behind you on that. I promise that as soon as I get back to the real world, I will never stomp another spider, real or plastic, as long as I live, but until then, maybe you could just let me go? I've got to go rescue my annoying cousin from Big Bertha."

At my last two words, the spider reared back as if stung, front legs raised high in the air.

"Oh," I said, sitting up. "Thanks? Was it something I said? Big Bertha?"

The spider rubbed two of its legs against some bristles on its thorax, making a sort of whirring sound. I wasn't quite sure what that meant, but I took it as agreement.

"Has she tried to eat you?" I asked.

At this the spider reared again and then tapped its forelegs down on the surface of the trampoline, seemingly in a sort of pattern. Ripples spread out from the points of impact. I didn't know Morse code, or spider code, or whatever this was, but it was clear it was trying to communicate in some way.

"Well," I said, "um, me and my friend are going to try to make her stop eating people and arachnids and all. I just need to find her first."

This was sort of true. I mean, it wasn't our main goal, but at the very least we needed to convince her to cough up Mercy's grandfather. If that was even possible.

The spider gave a small, surprisingly delicate hop and

then scuttled away in the direction it had come. After a few feet it paused, glancing back at me.

I realized, with surprise, that I genuinely wasn't afraid of it anymore. I climbed to my feet and followed.

When we reached the edge of the trampoline, it gestured urgently with a leg. I squinted into the nothingness. At first, I couldn't see anything. But then I shifted my head a little and I spotted it: a glint of light shooting into the distance.

I knelt and peered closer. Attached to the side of the trampoline was a web, almost invisible unless you stared at it from exactly the right angle. It stretched out through the air, into the void.

The spider performed a complex mime, waving its many legs, its many sneakers. I was pretty sure I understood: it wanted to help.

The spider waited by the web while I went to retrieve Uncle Steven. He was huddled in the farthest corner of the trampoline, his shirt pulled over his head, apparently trying to hide.

"Hey," I said when I got close, "everything is fine now."

"Is the spider gone?" he asked, voice muffled.

"No," I glanced back across the trampoline. "But don't worry, it's a friendly spider."

"Friendly?" Uncle Steven emerged from his shirt to glare at me. "Spiders aren't friendly! They're insects! Nasty insects with poison and too many legs."

"Arachnids, actually."

"What?"

"They're arachnids," I said, "not insects. But look, it doesn't matter. We should go find Jake and Mercy. The spider won't hurt you, I promise."

I don't know why I was so sure of it, but I was. Perhaps the very fact that I was so sure of it was enough to make it true. If that makes any sense. Which it doesn't.

It took several more minutes of convincing to get Uncle Steven to approach the spider, and even then I had to tug him by the arm for the last few feet.

"You," he said, pointing a trembling finger at the spider, "had better not crawl across my face or I don't know what I'll do."

"It's not so big on crawling across people, as far as I can tell," I said. "It prefers stomping them."

The spider shuffled its feet abashedly.

Uncle Steven shook his head. "They did not prepare me for this in business school." He glanced over at the nothingness beyond the trampoline and then quickly looked away. He clearly hadn't seen the web yet. "Now, how do I find my son?"

The spider knelt, improbably, despite its distinct lack of knees. It lowered its head until it was almost touching the fabric of the trampoline.

"What's it doing now?" Uncle Steven asked, backing up a step.

"You're not going to like this," I told him.

"I'll bloody well love it if it gets us off this blasted trampoline."

So I told him. His face went red as an apple and he gulped, but he couldn't very well take it back now, could he?

HOW A FLY FEELS

The spider scurried along the web with the two of us astride its back. The bristly hairs on its side tickled my ankles. It was much more solid than the inflatable animals, which was reassuring, and it wasn't actually moving through thin air. Every now and then I would catch a glimmer of web beneath us, but even when I couldn't see it, I trusted it was there.

I'd read once that spider silk, as delicate as it may appear, is actually among the strongest materials in the world, stronger even than steel. I focused on this fact.

The mere fact that I believed it was probably enough to make it true, here.

The spider was remarkably agile for its size. We moved with great speed across the empty landscape, or skyscape, or nothing-scape, or whatever it was.

I had a pretty good idea of where to find Jake. So, unpleasant though the prospect was, we were headed to Bertha.

I was afraid of this, but I was doing it anyway. My mother would call that brave. I'd call it a terrible idea. But I wanted to redeem myself.

The spider seemed to know which way to go, and it wasn't long before the voluminous shape that was Bertha appeared in the distance. Her voice rumbled out like a clap of thunder that had just seen a particularly excellent performance from its favorite band. The web swayed in the breeze of her exhaled breath.

The spider paused. It seemed hesitant to get any closer.

She was even bigger than she had been last time I saw her, though that couldn't have been more than an hour or two ago. She was gripping a section of blue plastic tubing, crunching on it like a carrot.

"What's going on?" asked Uncle Steven from behind me. He leaned around me to get a better view. "Oh! She's one of the games!"

Perhaps Bertha heard him—her ears were now the size of canyons—because she turned.

Her black plastic eyes were darker than coal, darker than a raven's wings, darker than the darkest dark thing I'd ever seen in a poorly lit basement room on an overcast day. At their edges they were that dark, and they just got darker and darker toward the centers. They were so dark they almost came full-circle back to being bright.

Those eyes focused on us.

"Ah," she exclaimed. "More of you."

The spider bolted. I couldn't really blame it. Uncle Steven and I tumbled from its back. Luckily, we didn't fall far, as we were immediately caught by the thin sticky fibers of the web we'd been traveling along.

I tried to sit up, but my legs and arms were stuck fast to the web. I twisted and struggled, only managing to get myself more tightly ensnared. Uncle Steven was suspended to my left, though he'd managed to land in a seated position, so only his legs were stuck.

Bertha lifted her left arm, reached toward us.

I closed my eyes, took a deep breath. I'd had success with the spider, so why not Bertha? Maybe she, too, was only monstrous if I thought of her as a monster.

"Hello, um, ma'am," I called out, opening my eyes. "How are you doing this fine day?"

She cocked her head, lowered her arm. "I am very hungry," she said. "Nothing I eat satisfies the hunger. It is endless. An ache. An ocean inside me that has been drained. The endlessness of what you call space." She blinked at me. "Will you tell me about space? More than anything else, I crave to understand your world."

"Yeah," I called. "Totally, I'll give you a full accounting

of the solar system, everything you ever wanted to know, if you could just help me with one small thing."

"Very well," said Bertha.

Beside me, Uncle Steven was tugging frantically at his pants legs, trying to get free of the web.

"There's this guy Jake," I shouted. "He looks a bit like me, but taller. Brown hair."

"Ah yes," she said. "He was very unpleasant. Wouldn't tell me any stories."

My heart sank. "Well, the thing is, I need to find him. He's my cousin."

Uncle Steven piped up for the first time. "And my son."

"I am sorry." Bertha swung her gaze over to Uncle Steven. "He must be a great disappointment to you."

Uncle Steven ignored that. "Where is he?"

"I ate him," said Bertha.

"What?!"

"I was very hungry," said Bertha, calm and matter-of-fact. "So I ate him."

Uncle Steven fainted.

HOW A
SANDWICH FEELS

So much for not being scared of Bertha. My matter overcame my mind, and I was suddenly and violently terrified. I squeezed my eyes shut, wished desperately that I was anywhere but here, completely trapped with my unconscious uncle and a woman who had just casually admitted to the probable murder of my cousin.

"I leave you alone for *one* second," said Mercy.

The shock of her voice caused my eyes to snap open of their own accord.

Mercy was hovering just a few feet to the right of the web, astride the inflatable bear. To her right floated the lion from last time.

And sitting atop the lion was, well, *also* Mercy.

I blinked hard, eyes flicking back and forth between the two Mercys. At first glance, they appeared identical in every way except their rides.

"Three of you now," Bertha said. There were four of us

by my count, but maybe she meant three real people. Because one of the two Mercys was a fake.

Mercy—the one on the bear—flew a little closer to the web and prodded the prone form of Uncle Steven in the side with her foot. He jolted awake with a noise halfway between a gargle and a scream and clutched at his chest.

"Is he okay?" asked the Mercy sitting on the lion. "Is he having a heart attack?"

"Wouldn't be surprised," I said, "given the number of mozzarella sticks he ate."

Uncle Steven caught his breath. "That woman ate my child!" he cried.

Bertha had been watching the proceedings with interest.

"You must tell me," she said. "What it is like to have a child? How does it feel? Come closer."

She reached toward us again.

Uncle Steven yelped. The two Mercys moved in unison, swooping in and grabbing one of his arms each. They yanked and he popped free of the web.

Which was great for him. But not so great for me.

Because now, when Bertha's hand closed around the section of web he'd just been stuck to, the only person there was me.

I told myself she wasn't real. I told myself this web wasn't real. None of it was. I could change it. I could control it.

But it was no use. My heart hammered in my chest as I was ripped bodily from the web. Stronger than steel or not, the spider silk proved little obstacle to Bertha.

I landed on the expansive hill at the base of her thumb and then tumbled down into the valley of her palm.

A rush of air pinned me motionless as Bertha lifted her hand, with me on it, to her mouth. Her face drew nearer and, with it, her eyes. This close, I would swear I could see the hunger in them. Like a black hole, the death of a star. Galaxies were being torn apart in the depths of that shiny plastic.

Bertha opened her mouth. Her teeth rose up like jagged skyscrapers. I could feel the heat of her breath as it gusted out of her lungs.

"Tell me everything," she said.

I admit that all I managed at this point was a terrified squeak.

Her eyes pivoted past me. I followed her gaze and saw the bear and the lion swooping closer.

"Mercy," I shouted. "Help!"

I scrambled to my feet and ran across Bertha's palm.

Bertha narrowed her eyes. Her fingers curled up, blocking my path.

"I am hungry," she said.

With a casual flick of her wrist, she tossed me into her mouth as easily as a piece of popcorn. I soared through the air and landed on a spongy, undulating mass—her tongue. I grabbed a handful of taste buds and tried to pull myself away from her gnashing teeth.

Then she must have swallowed. A wave of saliva cascaded over me. It was like a water park slide except grosser and slimier and infinitely more terrifying. I was swept up and carried down her throat, into darkness.

JONAH AND JONAH
AND THE WHALE

I fell through the darkness and then suddenly I stopped. As far as I could tell I hadn't actually landed. It felt as though I was just suspended in midair, as if time itself had ground to a halt.

I couldn't see anything. I was aware of a burbling, splashing sound from somewhere far below. I'm not sure how long I hung there, afraid to move in case I fell again. My blood buzzed with fear, my skin prickled with the anticipation of being dissolved by acidic bile and digestive enzymes.

The darkness was easier to deal with if I kept my eyes closed. That way I could at least pretend that when I opened them again it would be gone.

And indeed, when I next opened my eyes, two tiny lights had appeared off to my left, weak and flickering but unmistakably there. As I watched, one of the lights grew steadily larger, bobbing up and down in the darkness.

My fear swelled. My blood pounded in my ears. Was this the approach of death? Should I turn away from the light?

And then I heard the voices.

"What is it?" called the first voice. It was faint, far in the distance. "Anything useful?"

The voice echoed strangely in the gloom. It sounded familiar, too, incredibly familiar, though I couldn't tell who it was. Nonetheless, I was instantly comforted. My situation might be dire, but at least I wasn't alone.

"Not sure yet," said a second voice, much louder. This one I had no trouble identifying.

"Uncle Steven?" I croaked out.

"What?" he said. "Is something wrong?" and in another moment I could see him, his face illuminated dimly by the small flashlight he held. "Where are you?"

"I'm here," I gasped. Impulsively I jerked my arm up to wave at him and signal my location, but my arm was stuck. I could move it only a few inches and then it snapped back to where it had been before.

Uncle Steven turned toward my voice and moved jerkily in my direction. He progressed slowly, staring down at his feet. The beam of his flashlight wobbled, and beneath him tiny glints of light shot off in all directions like fireworks. I realized all at once why I had stopped. It made sense. It made so much sense that I was surprised I hadn't thought of it before.

I was caught in another spiderweb.

Back in the real world, the spider-stomping game had a total of eight small arachnid-shaped pedals for children to stomp. So it would make sense if there were at least eight giant spiders here. I guess this explained where the other six had gone.

Uncle Steven continued to move haltingly toward me. His progress, I saw now, was so slow because with each step he had to wrench his foot free from the sticky grip of the web while at the same time being very careful not to topple over.

When he had nearly reached me, he turned the flashlight beam full in my face. I blinked.

"What are you doing down there?" he demanded.

"What do you mean what am I doing? Bertha ate me! I thought maybe you and the Mercys got away, but I guess not. Where are they?" I peered into the darkness, feeling very confused.

And I'm sorry to say it, but I was about to get way more confused.

Uncle Steven crouched down, flashlight still pointed right at my face. He stared at me, his brow creased and eyes in deep shadow.

"Uh, a little help here, maybe?" I suggested.

"Nathan?" he asked.

"What?" I thought he would have been glad to see me. I was certainly glad to see him.

Out in the darkness, someone shouted Uncle Steven's name.

"I'm here!" Uncle Steven called, standing up, moving the flashlight beam off my face, finally. I blinked hard at the afterimage of the light.

"Is everything okay?" It was that first voice I had heard. If I squinted, I could see the second light flickering in the darkness.

"I'm fine," called Uncle Steven. "But you're going to want to see this."

The light moved closer and closer and then it was so close that I could see it originated from a novelty lamp shaped like a rubber duck.

The person holding the lamp was making their way carefully toward us. The yellow light of the duck was too dim for me to make out their face.

Uncle Steven gave an ear-splitting whistle.

"What's going on?" I asked. My panic was rising again. The web shook.

For a moment I didn't even notice that the owner of the duck lamp had reached us. He leaned down, holding out the duck to illuminate my face. As soon as he got a look at it, he startled and almost fell back onto the web. I would have done the same if I hadn't already been there.

Because, of course, *he* was me.

COPYCAT

"Hi," said me.

"Hi," I said.

"Just what I need," muttered Uncle Steven. "*Two* of them."

It was not like looking into a mirror, not at all. When you look into a mirror and smile, your reflection will smile back. I had no idea what this other me would do. He was no reflection—he was a three-dimensional being who could move and speak and make terrible puns.

"Nice of you to have dropped in," he said. His voice was slightly different than the voice I heard when I spoke. I figured I must be hearing, for the first time, exactly what I sounded like to other people.

Uncle Steven—although he wasn't really my uncle, I realized now, but a fake Nowhere-version of him—whistled again and stared out into the void. "Where are they?" he asked the fake me, who shrugged.

Something prodded me gently in the shoulder. I whipped my head around and found myself staring at the toe of a bright blue high-top sneaker. I didn't even have to look up to know what sort of leg it would be connected to.

This spider was even larger, it seemed, than the ones I had met out on the trampoline. Behind it I could barely make out the hulking shape of a second spider, itself even larger than the first. I concentrated very hard and managed, barely, not to scream.

"Here they are," I whispered instead.

"Ah," said Fake Uncle Steven, addressing the spiders. "Took you long enough."

If the spiders gave any kind of response to that, it was lost to me because the web began to shake again, violently, and with it came a great rumbling, roaring noise that reverberated around my skull and shook my ribs.

The noise subsided quickly, although it was a good minute or so before the web was entirely still.

"What in the hell was that?" I asked, although as soon as I asked it became clear to me. What else could it be? I'd heard Bertha speaking before, just not from the inside.

"You're not in hell," said the fake me. "You're just in a stomach."

"Well, yes, I know."

A slight tremor ran through the web, much less violent than the voice-quake. One of the two spiders loped off into the blackness.

"Hope it's something useful this time," said Fake Uncle Steven.

"Sorry to bother you," I said, "but I could use a teensy bit of help here."

"Oh, sorry," said fake me. "I thought you were just *hanging out* down there."

"Right," I said, resisting the urge to roll my eyes. I wasn't this annoying in real life, was I? That hadn't even been funny. "Seriously, though, a little help?"

The two of them crouched and grabbed onto my arms, while the spider that had stayed carefully snipped the web around me using its jagged mouthparts. As soon as I was free, they hauled me over to where the web was still intact and propped me up on my feet.

It was a good thing they still had me by the arms, because the web started quaking again, the darkness reverberating with the roar of Bertha's voice, and I nearly fell over. It was loud from the outside, but absolutely deafening in here.

"This happens a lot," Fake Uncle Steven shouted over the din. "You just have to get used to it."

I had no desire to get used to it. I had a great desire to get away from it forever.

When the shockwaves subsided, the spider began to repair the web. It was fascinating to watch it work, and not just because of its size. I'd never seen a spider spinning a web before. I'd never really thought about how they managed it. It turns out that the silk comes out of the spider's back end—like, it is basically *pooping* silk— and yet it managed to make the activity look quite graceful. Majestic, even. Nothing that could be described as majestic ever comes out of humans' back ends.

Another slight tremor ran through the web.

"What was that?" I asked my fake self.

"That means something got caught in the web," my fake self explained.

"Another person?" I asked.

My fake self shrugged.

"Could be," I said. "Or a hunk of plastic. We've been getting a lot of those lately."

"I feel like I've lost my marbles," I said. "Talking to myself."

"I know exactly what you mean," I said.

"I guess you would," I said.

"Better than anyone," I said.

I AM LARGE,
I CONTAIN MULTITUDES

The spider finished patching up the me-shaped hole in the web and then headed off into the darkness.

"How about you take your evil twin here back to camp," Fake Uncle Steven said to Fake Nathan (Nathan 2.0? Nathan, the sequel?).

"Camp?" I asked. "Oh geez, just wait until Rudy hears about this."

"Who?" asked Fake Nathan.

I blinked at him, surprised.

He stared back at me, not blinking, with a look of intense concentration.

"Oh right," he said suddenly. "Of course. My best friend. Rudy. Just wait until he hears about this!"

He turned away and walked off into a patch of blackness totally indistinguishable from the rest of the blackness around it. I followed carefully.

"How can you tell where we're going?" I asked.

"Can't you see it?" Fake Nathan pointed to some vague point in the lightless distance.

"What am I supposed to be seeing?"

"It's brighter there," he said.

I couldn't see a thing, but Fake Nathan told me not to worry about it.

"It'll probably take about half an hour before your eyes fully adjust," he said. "After a while you'll get really good at telling different kinds of darkness apart."

My eyes were indeed starting to adjust a bit by the time we reached the rope ladder. It descended from a neat hole in the web and it, too, was spun from spider silk.

I descended it hesitantly at first, afraid of breaking the glittering strands that constituted the rungs of the ladder. But the spider silk had been holding our weight this whole time, and probably more besides.

At the bottom of the ladder was another web. The weaving here was so thick that there were barely any gaps between the strands. The silk wasn't sticky, either, so it was easy to walk along it.

Fake Nathan climbed down, too, bringing the light of the duck with him. I could just make out gray shapes in the darkness—structures like crooked tents—lumpy and leaning in all directions.

As we walked closer, I saw that the tents were cobbled

together out of a variety of junk—mismatched shoes, Styrofoam plates, ragged chunks of colored plastic—and held together loosely by spider silk.

"Hey, everybody," shouted Fake Nathan. "Come see the new guy."

People started to emerge like ghosts from the shadows around us. Some considerably more like ghosts than others, as many of them were varying degrees of transparent.

I was quickly surrounded by see-through children. I'm not sure how they could tell that between the two of us I was the new guy, but they obviously could. They poked me in the knees and bombarded me with questions.

"Where did you come from?"

"What's your favorite color?"

"How old are you? I'm five!"

I spotted a face I recognized. There was a kid up at the front, somewhat more substantial than his peers, who was the spitting image of the kid I'd dragged out of the ball pit two days ago—Brayden, was it?

Shadows hovered at the far edges of the crowd. I say shadows, but they weren't the sort of shadows cast by light. They were more like a disturbance in the air, the shimmer above a hot pavement, a different kind of darkness.

"What are those?" I whispered.

The other Nathan followed my gaze. "Oh, *those*," he said. "Those are parents. Just ignore them."

John the security guard—who was neither shadow nor transparent—pushed his way through the crowd of children and shook my hand.

"Welcome," he said, smiling broadly.

Despite his relative opacity, I felt pretty sure that this John, much like the Uncle Steven I had met on the web, wasn't real. I scanned the crowd for Jake or Mercy's grandfather. I had survived being consumed, so hopefully they had, too.

Fake Nathan handed the duck lamp off to Fake John, who headed up the ladder.

"It's his turn to patrol the catching web," Fake Nathan explained to me. "We take it in shifts. Once you get settled in, you'll get a shift, too."

I wasn't planning to get settled in—I was planning to get the hell out of here as soon as possible—but I chose not to mention it. I didn't want to offend myself.

"Come on," said Fake Nathan. "I want to show you my house."

INCOMPLETE
MIMESIS

It wasn't a house at all, of course, just another one of those lopsided junk tents. Still, once I was inside, I had to admit it was almost cozy. The walls were made of pieces of plastic fitted together like a tile mosaic, with occasional glow-in-the-dark star accents. There was enough space in the tent for us to stand comfortably and it was furnished with two inflatable chairs—an upper-tier prize-counter offering.

"Aren't these neat?" said Fake Nathan, flopping down onto one of them. "I was thrilled when Bertha ate them."

"Uh, yeah. Totally." I wasn't quite sure how to talk to him. He was sort of me, but sort of not. Did he even know that he wasn't real? Would asking that be rude?

"So does the web catch everything that Bertha eats?" I asked, instead.

Fake Nathan shook his head. "No way. She's been growing way too fast for the spiders to keep up. The web only stretches like a third of the way across—plenty of stuff misses it entirely."

That gave me a sick feeling in the pit of my stomach. How close had I come to missing?

It was with great unease that I asked my next question. "So, my cousin Jake . . . Bertha ate him, too. Have you seen him?"

"Oh yeah," said Nathan brightly. "He's a jerk. Really seems to hate me for some reason."

I breathed out, relieved. Nathan was right, Jake could be a jerk, but that didn't mean I wished him dead.

"So he's here?"

"Yeah, both of him."

Which made way more sense to me than it had any right to do.

"What about Mercy's grandfather?" I asked.

Fake Nathan looked confused, so I described to him the old man I'd seen the day before.

"Nope," said Fake Nathan. "No one like that around here."

My heart sank. What did that mean? Was Mercy's grandfather actually dead for real this time? Or had he made it out somehow? I wished Mercy were here so I could ask her what she thought.

For now, though, it was up to me.

The two Jakes, I learned from Fake Nathan, lived at opposite ends of the camp, as far apart from each other as the limited real estate possibilities of the web allowed. It wasn't too difficult to establish which one I wanted to see.

"Apparently he was screaming when they found him," Fake Nathan said. "That's what Uncle Steven told me. He wouldn't stop screaming even after they got him back to camp. There was already a Jake there and when the new one saw him, he tried to punch him in the face. I'm glad you didn't do that when you showed up."

"I would never," I said, though the truth was I would have been tempted if he'd made any more puns.

At my request, Fake Nathan led me through the so-called camp. For the most part it was just a loose assemblage of junk-tents in various sizes, colors, and shapes. The smallest, most haphazard tents belonged to the transparent children, most of whom—according to the other Nathan—faded away entirely after a while.

"I used to be transparent myself, actually," he added.

"Wait, really?"

"Yup. And then one day: Bam! Solid!" He considered for a moment. "I guess it must have been that puberty thing people always talk about."

I laughed.

Fake Nathan shot me a sidelong glance, studying me. And then, a little too late, he laughed, too.

CAIN AND CAIN

Jake's tent was built almost at the very edge of the web, a ramshackle structure composed of mope, baking trays, and paper towels. When we reached it, the other Nathan hung back while I walked up to the tent and knocked on one of the trays that made up the walls.

A few seconds later Jake emerged, carrying a pink-and-orange Lava lamp. The cord dangled from the base, unplugged, but the lamp still cast a hypnotic liquid light, which I guess made as much sense as anything around here.

"I told you to leave me alone," Jake snapped.

"No," called the other Nathan from behind me. "You told *me* that."

I glanced back at him. He'd sidled farther away, apparently loath to come too close. When I turned back around, Jake was staring at me. Really *staring*, as though he was sizing me up for a fight. Lit from below by the Lava lamp, his features appeared menacing and jagged, like a jack-o'-lantern carved with an axe.

"You're real," he said suddenly.

"I am?" I asked, startled. "I mean, yes, I am."

At this his face sort of crumpled, like a jack-o'-lantern kicked by some kids, and I was afraid he was going to start crying.

"You really are, aren't you?" he said. "You've got to be, because there's two of you and there's two of me and one of me is real, aren't I? I've got to be."

"What?"

Jake leaned forward and grabbed my shirt.

"You've got to get me out of here," Jake said. "I can't take it anymore."

And then he really did start to cry.

I stood there awkwardly.

"Uh, there, there," I mumbled, and patted his arm.

My cousin had never cried in front of me before, even when we were younger. He always acted tough—and sometimes even downright mean.

Jake let go of my shirt and wiped his face with his sleeve. Then he let out a stream of curse words the quantity and diversity of which were frankly impressive. That seemed to make him feel better.

A gaggle of transparent kids, drawn no doubt by the undeniable allure of foul language, had appeared and were watching us.

"Get out of here," Jake shouted at them. "Scram. You creepy little weirdos."

He brandished the Lava lamp. They scattered.

And I saw right through Jake—I mean, not literally, the way I could see through the kids. But I saw something I hadn't before—all his bravado was just a way of hiding, of covering it up when he was scared or upset, the same way I sometimes covered up being scared with silly jokes.

"Ugh," he said. "They're awful."

"They seem okay to me."

Jake snorted. "Here, come on, I want to show you something."

He strode off purposefully across the web. I had to almost run to keep up with him. He darted among the tents until he reached a big one, which seemed to be storage for all the items scavenged from the upper web. Inside, he moved from pile of junk to pile of junk until he found what he was looking for—a long, jagged shard of bright red plastic.

"What is it?" I asked. "What are you showing me?"

"Just come on," he said, and headed back out.

I followed him until we reached a tent made of mops, baking trays, and paper towels. It looked exactly like Jake's tent. For a moment I thought we'd gone in a big circle, but when Jake banged on one of the baking trays, a voice came from inside.

"Go away," it said.

"No," said Jake.

He hammered on the baking tray until the owner of the voice appeared at the entrance to the tent. It was, of course, also Jake. Fake Jake had no Lava lamp and no big shard of red plastic, but otherwise the two were identical.

Fake Jake opened his mouth to say something, but he never got a chance because Real Jake lifted the shard of plastic high into the air and then plunged it deep into Fake Jake's chest.

MURDER MOST CONFUSING

F ake Jake gaped at the plastic protruding from his chest and then crumpled to the web, his beige Krazyland staff shirt already beginning to stain with blood.

"What the hell did you do that for?" I shouted.

Real Jake just smirked.

I dropped to my knees next to the fallen Jake. I really had no idea what to do. Should I remove the shard of plastic? Or would that make it worse? In desperation I jammed my hands over the wound in a vain attempt to stop the blood. I wished again that Mercy were there. She would probably know what to do.

"He's faking it," said Real Jake.

Fake Jake let out a gurgle of pain. His eyes rolled back in his head.

"You're going to be okay," I said, pressing harder against the wound. "Just hold on."

"Stop it," said Real Jake.

"I'm not going to stop it," I yelled. "*You* stop stabbing people. Don't just stand there. Go get some help."

"I wasn't talking to you," said Real Jake calmly. He leaned down close to his fallen counterpart. "Stop it," he repeated. "Stop bleeding."

And, to my great surprise, Fake Jake promptly did.

Real Jake pushed me out of the way. I staggered back, too shocked to protest. Real Jake put his foot on Fake Jake's stomach and wrenched the plastic shard from his chest. Fake Jake sprang to his feet, gave us both the finger, and then darted back into the tent.

"See," said Real Jake. "Isn't he the worst?"

"He's you!" I spluttered, still recovering from the emotional whiplash. I'd forgotten that fake people weren't alive in quite the same sense we were—or at least they weren't animated by the same biological processes.

It was perhaps surprising that Fake Jake had even had blood. Perhaps he had been studying Jake, the same way that Fake Nathan seemed to be studying me, learning how to act more real.

"He's not me," insisted Jake. "He's copying me. It's like identity theft or something. He stole my face."

"Maybe," I conceded, "but that's no reason to go around stabbing people."

"He's not even people."

"Everybody is people," I said, glancing back at Fake

Nathan, who had followed us over here and was hovering in the shadows. Creepy or not, he still deserved a fair chance.

I felt another one of my mother's aphorisms creeping toward my tongue.

"And you should treat others the way you'd like to be treated," I told Jake. "Especially if they are literally your doppelganger!"

"Ugh," said Jake. "You aren't better than me just because you know big words, okay?"

"What?" I blinked at him, confused for a moment. "Oh, you mean *doppelganger*? It just means, like, your double or whatever."

"We get it, you read books. There's plenty of things I know more about than you."

Was Jake . . . insecure?

He'd said before we fell into the ball pit that I always had it out for him. Could it be possible he truly felt like I was the one who was mean to him?

"Look," I said. "I don't think I'm better than you because I'm—" I stopped myself just in time to keep from saying *smarter than you.*

Was I mean to Jake? I mean, I knew it sucked to be treated like you weren't smart. But even if I was guilty of doing that sometimes, it didn't justify his being mean back to me.

"—because I know a lot of words," I finished. "But you also aren't better than me just because you're older and taller."

Jake scowled but seemed to be considering his next words carefully. Maybe, just maybe, we were about to make a breakthrough.

"Nerd," he said.

THE OTHER
WAY OUT

My heart-to-heart with Jake was interrupted by the reemergence of Fake Jake from his tent, brandishing what appeared to be a mallet from the Whac-A-Mole game.

"Watch out!" I shouted.

Real Jake turned just in time to ward off a strike by his counterpart. The two began to grapple hand to hand, both cursing profusely. One of the Jakes insulted the other Jake's mother, a move which I suspected he hadn't fully thought through.

Why did Jake hate himself so much? It almost made me feel sorry for him.

A transparent kid, roughly the opacity level of lime Jell-O, came running up and tugged on the hem of my shirt.

"What is it?" I asked.

"New girl wants to talk to you," the kid said.

New girl? My heart leapt. A second later I leapt, too, to avoid the tangled form of the two Jakes. They had somehow managed to get each other in simultaneous headlocks and were now hurtling this way and that across the web.

"Let's go," I said, waving at Fake Nathan, and we departed hastily, leaving the Jakes to work things out for themselves.

Mercy was just descending the silk ladder when we reached it.

"Mercy!" I shouted, running toward her, overcome with relief.

She turned and smiled at me. My heart sank.

"Oh," I said, unable to keep the disappointment out of my voice. "It's *you.*"

I was sure the real Mercy would have scowled at me. This version clearly hadn't quite gotten the full knack of being her.

Perhaps it wasn't entirely kind of me to wish that the real Mercy were here instead, since that would have meant she, too, was trapped in a giant's stomach. Though I'd half hoped she might try to come save me.

"Mercy sent me in here," Fake Mercy explained. "To see if you were dead."

I guess that was better than nothing.

"He's not dead," supplied Fake Nathan helpfully.

"Well, in that case," said Fake Mercy, "I'm supposed to rescue you and your cousin."

I brightened at that. "Oh, awesome." I stared up at the darkness above us. "Did you bring any inflatable animals with you?"

"I tried," said Fake Mercy, with a rueful shake of her head, "but the lion popped itself on one of Bertha's teeth on our way in."

"Darn."

"There's always the other way," she said.

"The other way?"

She pointed straight down.

"Ah," I said, as realization dawned. "Right."

A few minutes later, the three of us stood at the edge of the web, peering down into absolute darkness.

"Has anyone ever gone down there?" I asked.

"Not that I know of," said Fake Nathan.

"What do you think we should do?" I asked the other two, but they both just stared at me. After a moment, Fake Mercy shrugged.

I thought about what Jake had said about the fake people. Even I had to admit it was a little disconcerting how they would mimic your mannerisms, how they would stare at you.

I glanced at the abyss again. Only the thin, but surprisingly strong, strands of the web I stood on kept me from tumbling down into darkness. Which gave me an idea.

We climbed up to the catching web and tracked down several of the giant spiders. The spiders stomped (gently) on Fake Nathan while I explained my idea, but they seemed to be on board. Jake was done murdering himself by then, so we collected him and returned to the edge of the web.

"Who wants to go first?" I asked.

"I'll go," said Jake. "Whatever is down there can't be any worse than here."

I wouldn't have bet money on that, myself, but I was happy to let him be the guinea pig. Fake Mercy and I coiled strands of sticky web—produced on the spot by the giant spiders—around his torso while Fake Nathan secured an impromptu miner's helmet—made of an upside-down mixing bowl and a flashlight—to Jake's head.

News of what we were planning had spread quickly across the web and a small crowd of onlookers had gathered to watch the proceedings.

"I bet there're demons down there," said a transparent child.

"I bet there's sharks," said another one.

A giant spider wearing hot pink high-tops thrummed its legs as if to say, *I bet there are a bunch of professional exterminators with rolled-up newspapers and spray cans full of pesticide.*

"Well," said Fake Nathan, with a smirk I recognized, "*I* bet there's a large intestine."

One of them turned out to be right.

SPELUNKING

Once Fake Mercy and I finished wrapping Jake in the web fiber, he looked a lot like an unlucky fly. The webbing around him, which was to act like a harness, was connected to another long piece of spider silk, not sticky but very thick, which we used to lower him over the edge of the web.

We did this slowly, assisted by the spiders. Some of the fake kids had decided to join in and hold on to the rope, too, though I doubted they were contributing much.

"See anything yet?" I shouted to Jake, who had already been mostly swallowed by the darkness.

"No. Lower me faster!"

We did.

"Augh, slow down!" cried the disembodied voice of Jake from far below.

Eventually we reached a happy medium. Every few minutes or so Jake would call up and say "Nothing yet," or "Keep going," or "I think it just goes on forever." His shouts started to get fainter and fainter until finally we couldn't hear him at all. Luckily, I had foreseen this eventuality and worked out a rudimentary code.

One tug on the rope from our end meant *What's up, are you still alive?* One yank from him meant *Yes, I'm alive, keep going.*

Two tugs from Jake, on the other hand, meant *I've found something interesting, stop lowering me for a bit.*

We immediately stopped as soon as this message came through. Two yanks from our end would have meant we'd run out of rope. As it turned out we had run out of rope, some time ago, but the spiders jumped in quickly and spun more, attaching it seamlessly to the rope we already had.

We waited in silence, gripping the silk rope tightly, waiting for another message. If there were three yanks, we would haul him back up so that he could report on what he'd found.

We didn't have to wait long. A few moments later there was a short, sharp tug on the rope. We were about to start letting out more of it, but then there was another tug. And then another. And then one more. And then the rope started jerking wildly, with no apparent rhyme or rhythm.

"What is that supposed to mean?" yelled Fake Nathan, as he struggled to keep his hold on the leaping rope.

"Better pull him up," said Fake Mercy.

On the count of three we all heaved at the rope.

"Again!" called Mercy.

We heaved again.

The rope heaved back.

Next second, I found myself flying through the air, gripping the rope for dear life as I hurtled into the darkness below.

"Not again!" I cried, although since I was being yanked from the web as I said it, it came out more like "Not agaaAAAAAAAAAAAAAAHHHHH!"

THE SEA INSIDE

My fall was broken this time not by a trampoline or plastic balls or web but by liquid. I splashed into what I could only assume was stomach acid and began to flail, sure that any second my skin would start melting off.

I was holding my breath, but some of the liquid that surrounded me went up my nose and I switched fears. Now I was pretty sure I was going to drown.

I kicked my legs and waved my arms and somehow managed to generate enough panic-fueled force to propel myself upward. I broke the surface, coughing and spluttering. The liquid I was bobbing in surged like the ocean. Some of it splashed into my mouth and I realized it wasn't acid at all. It wasn't water, either.

It was oil.

I heard splashing somewhere nearby and Jake's voice. "Help!" he screamed. "Chicken wing!"

Which just made no sense whatsoever.

I struggled to keep my head above the surface. A wave broke over my head and I gulped down another mouthful of oil. It was salty, like seawater, with a distinct hint of bread crumbs.

When I surfaced again, everything had gone white. A beam of light shone directly in my eyes, so bright it hurt.

The light flashed off. The light flashed on again. Off. On.

The intermittent strobing illuminated the glistening oil ocean I was floating in. I glimpsed a dark shape moving beneath the surface. Something large. Big as a shark.

Desperately, I paddled away from the shape.

"Help!" I heard Jake shout again, and then another voice that I didn't recognize.

"Grab the rope!" it shouted.

Something hit the surface of the oil beside me. In the next flash of light, I saw that it was indeed a rope, made not of spider silk, but of hundreds of paper napkins knotted together. I grabbed on and was towed toward the strobing light.

My eyes were clouded with neon afterimages. Hands reached down from above, helped me up and onto a solid surface. The surface rocked beneath me like the deck of a boat.

Once my vision cleared, I saw that it was, in fact, a boat. A miniature strobe light (500 tickets at the prize counter) blinked on and off, outlining the curved bow of the boat. A man was kneeling on the deck, throwing out the napkin-rope again. His long gray beard dangled nearly to the oil. The strobe light glinted off his round glasses.

It was him. The one we'd come here to find. Mercy's grandfather.

The scene came to me in flashes thanks to the strobe light. A figure floated out in the oil sea, hair streaming out behind her. Fake Mercy. *Flash.* Gerald was pulling her closer. *Flash.* He was helping her up onto the boat. *Flash.* She was settling down cross-legged beside me on the deck, apparently unfazed by the whole ordeal.

The boat was peculiar. The deck seemed to be made of cardboard. Peering closer I saw that it was printed with nutritional info and ingredients. A frozen-pizza box.

The mast, meanwhile, was a bundle of oversize plastic straws and the sails seemed to be—no, surely not.

I stared hard at them in the next flash of light and sure enough, each sail was an enormous slice of pizza.

The oil made a sort of sense now. There was a kitchen in Krazyland, after all, complete with deep fryer. Nowhere must have tried to copy that kitchen, and Bertha, unsurprisingly, must have eaten the whole thing.

Gerald was throwing out the rope again. I climbed unsteadily to my feet and stumbled over to him.

"Help!" Jake's voice shouted from somewhere in the distance.

"Stop dillydallying and grab the rope," Gerald shouted back, "these are infested waters."

I reached the cardboard railing and saw, in the next flash of light, what he meant.

A deep-fried wing sliced through the oil, breaded coating glistening. It had, to my surprise and horror, a mouth. Full of teeth.

I supposed it was like the spiders. Here, the rules had gotten all mixed up. In Nowhere, chicken wings eat you.

DEAD MEN DO TELL TALES

The three of us on the boat managed to haul Jake to safety. He collapsed on the deck, muttering something under his breath about "teeth, so many teeth." The silk harness thread was still wrapped around his middle, but the thick rope that we'd used to lower him had snapped. Or perhaps been bitten through. It trailed limply on the deck beside him like an umbilical cord.

There was no sign of Fake Nathan and I was worried he hadn't made it, but then a shoal of mozzarella sticks darted through the oil to the left of the boat and I spotted, just beyond them, a hand reaching up out of the oily depths.

"Look!" I shouted, pointing.

The hand disappeared under the waves. Gerald threw the rope out again for the hand to grasp. When it failed to do so, Gerald plunged into the oil himself.

Beside me, Fake Mercy coughed up a small fish made of bread crumbs. It flopped about on the deck next to her feet. Jake made a faint whimpering noise and scooted rapidly away from the tiny fish as though he expected it to bite him.

Gerald reappeared, pulling himself over the side of the boat with one arm and dragging Fake Nathan along with the other.

Behind him, a chicken wing surged out of the oil, mouth agape, bristling with jagged hunks of enamel suitable for tearing flesh from bone as easy as a hot knife through terrified butter.

Gerald scrambled aboard just in time to avoid evisceration. The chicken-wing shark began to ram the side of the boat with its breaded snout.

Gerald dumped Fake Nathan on the deck and shouted a series of nonsensical phrases.

"Hoist the jig leeward! Batten the hatches! Trim the main! Lower the daggerboard! Ready the lazy sheet! Watch the boom! Jibe-ho! Tighten the gooseneck! Untangle the foul! Course to steer! Tacking starboard! Bear away!"

A series of creak and clicks echoed around me as the boat itself followed the man's strange orders. The pizza sails unfurled. An anchor made of a cast-iron pan hauled itself up and clanked onto the deck.

A moment later the sails caught Bertha's breath and we were off, sailing at top clip through the eternal night of the great gastrointestinal sea.

Gerald switched off the strobe light. We were plunged briefly into darkness before he lit a small lantern. Well, not so much a lantern as a square slice of sheet cake with icing roses and several birthday candles. But the effect was the same.

"Well," he said, "that was fun."

"Gerald?" I said. "Gerald Riverbottom?"

He froze, staring at me. He blinked hard, seemed to see me for the first time. A strange look came over his face. Recognition. And just for an instant: fear.

"No," he said. "You must be mistaken."

ENTIRELY FAKE

"**I**'m not mistaken," I told Gerald. "You're Mercy's grand-father. And you're real."

"Nope." His gaze flickered over to Fake Mercy and Fake Nathan for a moment, who were both standing placidly nearby. "I'm sorry to say I'm entirely fake."

I stared at him. He stared back, not blinking. He didn't seem to be breathing, either. I squinted at him. His eye twitched. His face was getting slightly red.

He gasped finally, drawing in a big breath.

"Ha!" I said, pointing an accusing finger.

"I was merely copying you," he said, with a devilish grin.

I sighed. This guy was maddening. That must run in the family. I looked to Fake Mercy for help, but she just shrugged. I wasn't sure if Real Mercy had filled her in on all our plans. Fake Nathan was peering over the side of the boat. Jake was huddled by the mast with his hands over his face. It was up to me again.

"Fine," I said. "Mr. Fake Gerald, sir, can you help us get out of here?"

"Happily," he said. "I know an easy way out."

"You do?" I was taken aback.

"Yes," he said, eyes twinkling behind his round blue glasses. "Just swim for it!"

He spun around and shoved Fake Nathan so hard that he toppled over the side of the boat. Gerald turned around, hands outstretched, reaching for me.

I stumbled backward and fell.

"Mercy!" I shouted. "Help!"

Fake Mercy ran forward, but only managed to distract her grandfather briefly as he lifted her up and tossed her into the oil.

A moment later, Gerald grabbed for my arm. I dodged, but he managed to get a hold on my leg. He pulled me across the deck. I kicked and squirmed, trying to free myself, but it was no use.

Suddenly: a blur of motion. Something flying through the air, so fast I couldn't tell what it was in the dim candlelight.

Gerald jerked backward and let go of my leg. I scuttled away from him and then turned to look. He was clawing at his face, which was now covered in buttercream icing. Jake stood nearby, clutching the birthday candles in one hand and the empty cake plate in the other.

For a moment I was too stunned to move. Jake had actually helped me.

Gerald roared with anger, stumbling and flailing, eyes still bleary with icing.

I jumped to my feet, grabbed the rope made of paper napkins, and threw one end over to Jake. He gave me a quick nod and then we both ran forward.

Gerald lunged for me but I dodged to the left and yanked the rope taut. He tripped, falling to the deck. Before he could get back up, Jake and I wrapped the rest of the rope around him and tied it tight.

"Thanks," I said to Jake, as Gerald wriggled fishlike at our feet. "You saved me."

"Nah." Jake shrugged, looking sort of embarrassed.

"Thanks anyway."

We turned our attention to rescuing the two fakes who Gerald had thrown overboard. Their presence in the oil had attracted the sharks again, but we managed to pull them back onto the boat before any of them got eaten.

Well, eaten *again.*

SPIN CYCLE

"I have no idea what to do now," I said. We were all sitting around in a circle on the deck, keeping an eye on Gerald. The four of us had pulled off some gluey strings of mozzarella from the sails and used those to wrap him up even more firmly and cover his mouth so he couldn't shout at us. He'd given up struggling and resorted to simply glaring at us.

"All those books you read didn't prepare you for this, eh?" said Jake. It was sort of teasing, but less mean than his usual repertoire.

"Do you have any ideas?" I asked.

He considered. "I guess if we had a knife, we could try to cut through the stomach lining."

Reflexively, I clutched a hand to my own stomach, imagining my food trying to hack its way out. The queasy feeling the thought gave me led to another idea.

"What if we made her puke?" I asked.

"That's not the worst idea I've ever heard," said Fake Mercy. That did seem like the sort of thing the real Mercy might say, though in general the copy was considerably more upbeat. Maybe fake people were less irritable since they never had to deal with things like indigestion or not getting enough sleep.

"I think it's a great idea," said Fake Nathan. I appreciated the support. I'd always thought it would be cool to have a sibling who was my same age and had all the same interests as me. If I could forget the fact that he wasn't real, it was kind of like that.

"What makes people puke?" I asked.

"You," said Fake Mercy without missing a beat. She was really getting the hang of this.

"Stomach flu," suggested Fake Nathan. "When I had the flu, I puked every day for like a week."

I frowned at him. I'd had the flu, of course, but I was surprised he had that memory, when not long ago he'd seemed unsure who Rudy was. Maybe spending time around me was making him more *real*.

"You never had stomach flu," said Jake, as if reading my mind.

But not literally reading my mind, the way Fake Nathan seemed to be doing.

"Sure I did," Fake Nathan insisted. "When I was seven."

You were never seven, I wanted to say, but I stopped myself. Arguing about it wasn't going to help us.

"Booze," said Jake suddenly.

"What?" I blinked at him. He might be older than me, but he definitely wasn't old enough to drink.

"It makes people puke sometimes," he explained.

"Oh right." I considered this. We were on a ship, and pirates and sailors drank a lot in movies. It seemed unlikely that there would be any alcohol in this place since there was certainly none in the real Krazyland. "She's got a strong stomach, though. Otherwise she'd have gotten indigestion long ago. I mean, she drank a whole ocean's worth of oil."

"Wait," said Jake. "That's it! Remember when we all went to Aunt Cynthia's and played whirlpool?"

"Yes," said Fake Nathan and I at the same time. I frowned at him. This was getting a little annoying. Not like stabbing-level annoying. But still.

Aunt Cynthia had a round aboveground pool, and when we visited a few summers ago, all the cousins, including me, Jake, and Jenny, invented a game where we ran around in a circle really fast until our combined motion whipped the oil into a whirlpool. The adults eventually made us stop because too much oil was sloshing over the sides of the pool.

But we could slosh as much as we wanted now.

"How do we steer the boat?" I asked.

Jake waved a hand at the bound form of Gerald. "The weird old guy just kind of shouted at it."

"Excuse me, boat?" I said. "Could you sail around in a circle for us?"

Nothing happened. Gerald had been here a long time, so maybe he had gotten better at influencing the things around him.

"Yo, Boaty McBoatface!" shouted Jake. "Move your butt!"

I shot him a look. Surely that wouldn't help.

But to my great surprise, the pizza sail rustled a bit, greasily, at this.

"Okay," I said, a bit louder. "Um, get going? Circumnavigate!"

The boat drifted forward, moving in a circle.

"Heck yeah," shouted Jake. "Do it *Tokyo Drift*-style!"

The boat revved, somehow, and sped up, spinning in ever-tighter circles.

It was Fake Mercy who came up with the idea of using Gerald as bait. Maybe being around real people was affecting her, too, making her act more like I would expect the real Mercy to act. We pushed her grandfather to the back of the boat and tied him to the railing so that just his feet were dangling in the oil.

Now, as we sailed, dark shapes appeared in the oil behind us, lured by the promise of a bite-size toe snack.

Chicken-wing sharks. A soft-pretzel squid. Onion-ring octopi.

They followed us, swimming fast after the bait. Jake

shouted at the boat to floor it, and the boat sailed faster and faster. It was working. The motion of all the sea creatures and the boat churned the oil ocean into a huge whirlpool.

Going around in circles was starting to make me dizzy. I sank to the deck and then noticed that Gerald had managed to free himself from his bindings. Maybe one of the sharks had helped by biting through the rope. Either way I saw him heaving himself back up onto the deck and ripping the cheese from his mouth.

"Stop!" he shouted to the boat.

But it was too late.

My ears rang with the mother of all retching noises. The air convulsed. The oily ocean flew upward. We were all carried with it. There was no air, only oil. It oozed up my nose, slimed my eyes. My breath failed me and I blacked out.

IDENTITY THEFT

When I woke up there was a jellyfish on my head.

I opened my mouth, intending to shout, *Why is there a jellyfish on my head? Please someone, for the love of all that is holy, get it off me!* but all I got for my trouble was a mouthful of salty oil. I gagged, flailed, treading oil water to stay above the surface. I thought for a moment our plan hadn't worked, that I was still stuck in Bertha's stomach, but then I caught sight of her.

She loomed on the horizon like an iceberg. At least she no longer loomed up around me, but that was small comfort since it was obvious that she'd gotten over her indigestion pretty quickly. She was wading through the oil ocean that the world had become, grabbing everything that floated past her, plucking flotsam and jetsam and bits of drift-plastic from the oil and popping them right back into her mouth.

The jellyfish on my head flopped around. I reached up

to shove it off, only to discover that it was not a jellyfish at all but the stringy head of a mop.

"Grab on," shouted Fake Nathan.

He was a few feet away, floating on a raft made from remnants of Gerald's boat—one giant pizza slice. He had hold of the other end of the mop. I grabbed on.

Fake Nathan towed me in and helped me onto his cheesy raft. It seemed dubiously buoyant, as the crust was getting soggy with oil and breaking off in bits, but it was better than nothing.

"This is so weird," I said.

"What is?" asked Fake Nathan.

I blinked at him, unsure where to start. The ocean of deep-fryer oil? The pizza raft? Bertha? *Him?*

"All of it," I said, to save time.

"Oh."

"You don't think it's weird at all, do you?"

It wasn't really a question. He obviously didn't. He squinted at me and I swear I could almost see the cogs turning in his head. Recalibrating.

"Yes," he said slowly. "Now that you mention it— I guess it is weird."

"But you didn't think it was weird before. You didn't think it was weird until I told you it was. You're plagiarizing me!"

That wasn't really fair. I didn't want to be like Jake, taking my frustration with this situation out on an easy target.

Still, he *was* copying me. There was no denying it. In school, teachers were always giving lectures on how serious the crime of plagiarism was and how we'd be immediately expelled if we so much as thought about copying the words of another without at least ten quotation marks and a citation and a footnote and signed permission from our parents or guardians.

Fake Nathan tilted his head, studying me.

"I remember," he said. "Mrs. Hinton said that copying someone else's assignment was as bad as stealing a car."

"You've never met Mrs. Hinton."

"She was my fifth-grade teacher."

"She wasn't, though. She was *my* fifth-grade teacher."

"But I remember her."

"You only remember her because I remember her."

"But I remember . . . I remember . . ." he faltered and fell silent. He had a look on his face like he was searching for something.

"Look," I said. "I don't know how, exactly, but you've been stealing my memories. You never had the stomach flu and you never met Mrs. Hinton. You never even went to school."

Fake Nathan frowned.

"You aren't even real," I said.

Now he had a look on his face like a kicked puppy, and I immediately felt bad.

I looked away, guilt gnawing at me. After all, it wasn't

Fake Nathan's fault. I tried to look at it from his perspective. What would it feel like to be nothingness? To have no form, no consciousness, and then suddenly pop into existence?

I mean, I guess that happens to everybody, in the beginning.

Bertha had waded over to a section of neon green tubing that hung in the air. As I watched, she proceeded to snap it out of the air—what was holding it there in the first place I will never know—and bend it into an L shape.

She stuck the long end of the L into the oil. She stuck the short end into her mouth.

And then she drank.

All the oil rushed immediately toward the end of her makeshift straw. Everyone and everything currently floating around, including us, was dragged along with it.

Bertha was, it seemed, truly inescapable.

CANDY MORALITY

"We've got to move!" I shouted at Fake Nathan. He stuck the mop back into the oil and tried, with little success, to paddle our raft away from Bertha.

I could think of few fates less dignified than being sucked up a giant plastic tube like that kid in *Charlie and the Chocolate Factory*. You know, what's-his-name? He was the chubby one, so of course, as far as the book was concerned, that meant he was an insatiable chocolate glutton with zero self-control who deserved whatever was coming to him. That always seemed a bit unfair to me.

Was I doomed to share the same fate? Forget about Jake. Apparently, the universe itself was bullying me now.

The level of the oil ocean was rapidly dropping as Bertha slurped. In the distance I spotted a corn-dog whale breaching the surface. Astride its back was a small figure with flowing gray hair—Grandpa Riverbottom.

With a cry of *"Yeehaw"* he sped off toward the Skee-Ball mountain, which rose out of the oil ocean on the horizon.

"Can we steer that way?" I said to Fake Nathan. He redoubled his efforts with the mop.

Debris floated past us. I fished out the nearest piece— a Whac-A-Mole hammer—and started frantically paddling as well.

Our combined struggle was just enough to keep us from being pulled swiftly toward Bertha's makeshift straw. We weren't getting closer to her, but we weren't getting farther away, either.

This world was emptier than ever. The only visible landmarks, besides the sea below and the plastic-ball cloud above, were the mountain and Bertha, who was about the same size as the mountain by now. Which meant we had two options.

"Okay," I told Fake Nathan, "we need to go toward her."

"What? Oh, I see."

Our minds worked the same way, so I didn't need to explain. We paddled hard. It was easier now since we weren't going directly against the current.

With one final push, we pulled the raft up alongside Bertha herself and then jumped. The raft spun away from us, pulled by the suction of the giant straw. But we were safe, or as safe as we could be in the situation, clinging to the hem of Bertha's dress. The fabric was coarsely woven, each individual thread as thick around as rope, so it was easy to hook our fingers into.

I looked up. Bertha's dress filled my sight, soaring up and up like a sheer cliff-face topped by a horrifying harvest moon. From this angle I could see right up the twin caverns of her nose.

"Sorry I said you weren't real," I told Fake Nathan.

"It's okay. You're right. I'm not."

He looked so sad when he said it I felt a stab of sympathy for him.

And, I guess, by extension, for Bertha. Because she knew she wasn't real, too, didn't she? Before, she'd asked Jake to tell her about our world. She knew.

"I mean, it's okay," I said. "We can't all be real."

He gave a small, half-hearted smile. "I only figured it out recently."

That made me feel even worse. Spending time around me had made him self-aware. What must two years around Gerald have done to Bertha?

"I still think you're a cool dude," I said.

"Thanks," he said. "I think you're a cool dude, too."

We each let go of Bertha's dress with one hand just long enough to give each other a high five. It was perfectly synchronized. The platonic ideal of high fives.

The oil ocean was receding rapidly. The surface had been just below our feet when we first climbed onto Bertha's dress, but now it was several feet lower and rushing toward the straw even faster than before. A herd of plastic Whack-A-Mole alligators floated past, followed by a small fleet of measuring cups, followed by Jake.

"Hey!" I shouted at him. "Swim this way!"

Jake thrashed, sending up big splashes of oil, but not getting anywhere. The current was carrying him farther and farther away.

"Augustus Gloop," said Fake Nathan suddenly.

"What?"

"The kid in *Charlie and the Chocolate Factory.*"

"Oh."

"Don't worry, you'll make it to the end of the tour." Fake Nathan smiled at me. The smile was real, even if the face wearing it wasn't. "I really enjoyed being you."

Then before I could say anything in response, he let go of Bertha's dress and fell back into the oil.

THE OCEAN IS JUST A BIG MIRROR FOR BIRDS

watched myself swim out. I watched myself, my other self, my better self, maybe, pull Jake from the water and hoist him up so he could breathe, and then swim back toward Bertha, weighed down now with an already-heavy burden made more burdensome by its insistence on squirming and shouting.

When the two were within a yard of Bertha, Fake Nathan shoved Jake forward so he could grab onto her dress. Jake promptly did so, clinging to it like a frightened child to its parent's leg.

Fake Nathan moved to do the same, but without warning a swift eddy swirled around him and he was carried, quick and vicious, back out into open oil.

He didn't even try to swim back again. He just floated.

His eyes met mine and for an instant I swear I could see through them. I saw what he saw. Saw myself, my real self, hanging from Bertha's dress. I saw myself brighter and more vivid than I had ever appeared in any mirror or photograph. Everything else—Bertha, the oil, the speckled sky—appeared pale and faded next to the bright pinprick of color and light that was me. Jake, to the far left, a lesser star.

The boy I saw—me—looked so real, so solid. And for a second, I felt as Fake Nathan felt. I felt flimsy and barely there. I envied this boy across the water. I admired him, too. He was alive.

Simply, but undeniably, alive.

And then he and I and we lifted my and his and our hand as if to high-five despite the un-crossable distance. And he and I and we smiled at us and them and me and the distance was crossed.

I could no longer distinguish one pronoun from another. I could no longer distinguish one Nathan from the other. I would not have been able to diagram a sentence about what was happening. Heck, I could barely even compose a sentence about it.

Mrs. Hinton would have been ashamed.

But then, just as quickly as it had begun, it was over. Fake Nathan was nowhere to be seen. I suppose the current pulled him under, but to me it looked like he just dissolved into the oil. A Nathan-shaped ice cube in the sun. One second here, next second gone.

I stared at the spot where he had vanished. I felt dizzy. I felt slightly in awe, too. Fake Nathan had sacrificed himself to save the life of some guy he barely knew. Some guy who had always been kind of a jerk to him, in fact. I would not have done that.

But then again, I guess I would have. Because I just had.

A few moments later, all sound (including the sound of my own thoughts) was drowned out by a riotous slurping sound, like when somebody has gotten to the bottom of their milkshake but they can't bear to see it end so they desperately suck air through the straw until the glass is dry.

In this case, though, the glass was the world, and Bertha didn't let up until every drop of oil ocean was gone.

There were still a few things that had been too heavy to float lying about like beached whales—some pixelated dinosaurs, a few refrigerators, several of the strong man's barbell weights from the test-your-own-strength machine. A whale.

Bertha moved forward to pick them up, her dress billowing. I hung on tight. Jake was doing the same about ten feet over, a look of abject terror on his face.

I moved closer to him, grabbing handfuls of Bertha's dress and swinging like a monkey.

Jake did a double take worthy of a sitcom.

"But . . . you . . ." He tilted his head toward where Fake Nathan had disappeared, apparently unwilling to let go of Bertha's dress for even the half second needed to point.

"Nah," I said. "That was the copy."

"Oh. Huh." Jake scanned the horizon—if it could even be called that since there was absolute nothingness in practically every direction. "Wonder what happened to mine."

He'd sounded almost wistful. I thought he'd hated his copy with a fiery passion, but who knew. Probably my cousin would need some major therapy if we ever got out of this.

Bertha's dress billowed again. She'd finished off the refrigerators and was moving ponderously toward the Skee-Ball mountain.

She hadn't noticed us. From her perspective we would have been about the size and relative weight of burrs. But nobody walked around with burrs stuck to their clothes forever.

EVEREST MIGHT BE TALL, BUT AT LEAST IT HAS NO TEETH

Jake wasn't too happy when I told him we had to climb up Bertha's dress. He pointed out, correctly, that we would essentially be backtracking—moving closer to Bertha's treacherous cavern of a mouth when recently our only goal had been to get as far away from it as possible. But we needed to reach the plastic-ball cloud if we ever wanted to get out of here, so for now it was our best option.

I talked Jake through the process of moving along Bertha's dress. Luckily, the threads of the fabric were strong and provided ample handholds. Still, every twenty feet or so Jake would freak out and I would have to wait until he had calmed down, all the while trying to keep him from shouting too loudly.

I was secretly proud that I was better at climbing than he was, but because I am also a better person than him, I chose not to give him grief about it.

As we moved upward, we also circled around so that we were clinging to the back of Bertha's dress rather than the side.

"I'm slipping!" cried Jake.

"You're not."

"I am!"

I sighed and grabbed his shirt while he scrabbled at the weave of the dress. If my estimations were correct, we were currently somewhere in the region of Bertha's middle back, most likely a difficult spot for her to reach. Not that Bertha wasn't more than capable of adapting a jagged length of plastic tubing for use as back-scratcher, but it was best not to dwell on such things.

There was one question, though, that I couldn't help but dwell on: Where was Mercy?

What if she had left? Gone back to the real world and left me here to fend for myself.

A hint of panic swelled in my chest at the thought of this possibility. My arms began, all of a sudden, to ache.

When Jake and I finally reached Bertha's neck, the dress ended, and we were forced to perform a series of complicated acrobatic maneuvers in order to grab hold of her thick yarn hair and shimmy up it. I figured once we reached the top of her head, we'd be able to see most of the world, assuming there was any of it left that she hadn't eaten. If no immediate plans presented themselves, we could construct an SOS out of dandruff.

Once I reached the top, however, I couldn't see a thing. Bertha's hair surrounded me like a scarlet corn maze.

When Jake caught up, the two of us pushed forward through the endless tresses. Presently we stumbled onto a long, narrow clearing—the part of Bertha's hair.

"Who's that?" asked Jake. There was a figure ahead of us, standing in the center of the part. Beige shirt. Hands on hips. Hair the color of dirty bathwater.

"Mercy!" I shouted.

She turned and scowled at me. My heart felt light with relief. Was it her? The real deal? I moved forward, my arms held out as if to hug her.

Her eyes went wide and she backed away so fast that she tripped on a stray follicle and fell flat on her back.

Definitely the real one.

Jake started to laugh, but she turned her glare on him and he stopped abruptly.

I offered my hand to help Mercy up but, much like the very first time I'd ever met her, she regarded it as one might regard a dead fish and got to her feet on her own.

"It's good to see you," I said.

"Yeah, yeah," she said, then turned and called out "Mr. Clark!"

A few moments later Uncle Steven burst through the crimson hair-vines. As soon as he saw Jake, safe and more or less sound, his face lit up and he tackled his son in a big hug.

"Ugh, Dad. Stop it!" Jake squirmed away.

Now Mercy was the one laughing, Jake the one glaring.

"I was worried about you, son," said Uncle Steven.

"Whatever," said Jake.

Something bumped me in the back of the leg and I shrieked. When I turned, I saw it was just the inflatable bear, snuffling at the ground/scalp.

"We're down to just the one animal," said Mercy, "so we'll have to take turns when we leave. But first I need to figure out where the heck my grandfather is."

"About that—" I said, and then I gave her a short recap of what had happened down in Bertha's stomach. Jake chimed in a few times, too, highlighting his own extreme bravery.

"You let him get away?!" Mercy said, when we'd finished our tale.

"We didn't mean to."

Mercy sighed. "Maybe you three should head back now. He's *my* grandfather. I should be the one to deal with him."

"Are you sure?" asked Uncle Steven.

"Yes," she said. "It will honestly make my job easier if I don't have to worry about all of you getting eaten again."

Jake shivered a little.

"You want to go first, Nathan?" Uncle Steven asked, gesturing at the bear. Going home sounded great, but I could feel my knees getting ready to buckle at the mere thought of climbing aboard an inflatable animal again.

I considered coming up with some excuse, but then I shook my head and just went with the truth.

"I'm too scared," I said. "I'd rather someone else go first."

I saw Jake wrestling with himself, itching to call me a wimp. But I was pretty sure I saw something else, too. Jake was almost as scared as I was.

"Of course," I said. "My mother did always say that real bravery is being scared of something and doing it anyway."

Jake scoffed. "That's the cheesiest thing I ever heard. Fine, I'll show you how it's done."

He swung a leg over the bear, shouted "giddy-up," and the two floated up to the cloud.

"MORE," cried Bertha.

The sound reverberated up from below us and I stumbled as the ground/scalp suddenly tilted. I grabbed a cable-thick strand of hair and held on tight to keep from sliding.

"What's going on?" cried Uncle Steven. He was clinging to a strand of hair to my left.

"She must be moving," said Mercy.

Bertha's head continued to tilt this way and that, but the motion had a sort of a rhythm to it. A bobbing, jaunty rhythm, like someone strolling along at an easy pace.

Up above, Jake had reached the cloud, though we were rapidly moving away from him. I saw him stand and wriggle up into the plastic balls. For a moment, his legs dangled out from the bottom of the cloud. He kicked, dislodging several plastic balls, then shimmied up and out of view.

The bear was already zooming down back to us. Uncle Steven required very little convincing to go next.

"Come on," said Mercy, after he'd gone floating up into the sky. "Let's at least see where she's going."

The two of us crawled carefully along Bertha's part. She must have finished off the last remnants of the plastic tunnels, because when we reached the edge of her hairline, we could see she was approaching the Skee-Ball mountain.

"That's where your grandfather was headed last time I saw him," I said.

"Maybe I can wait until she gets close enough and then jump across," Mercy said.

A moment later, we watched as Bertha reached the mountain and snapped off the entire top half of it with ease. She held the peak upside down like an ice-cream cone. Then she scooped the rest of the Skee-Ball track up in one massive hand, the earth folding as easily as soft serve, and dumped it into the mountain-cone. Some of the gravity-defying boulders sat on top like cherries.

"Or maybe not," amended Mercy.

I spotted a tiny figure running along the edge of the mountain/ice-cream cone. He leapt from it onto the thumb that held the cone, and went running along Bertha's sleeve just as she took a bite.

And then the sky began to fall.

AWFUL ANCESTOR

A piece of sky hit Bertha's scalp a few inches from my foot and then rolled to a stop by my heel.

And when I say a piece of sky, I do, of course, mean a hollow plastic ball.

I looked up. Unfortunately, Bertha did, too. The ground/scalp tilted swiftly. Mercy and I clutched strands of hair and held on tight.

Uncle Steven had reached the ball cloud and stood balanced on the back of the bear.

Bertha roared with dismay, reaching up toward him.

"Uncle Steven, watch out!" I shouted, though I doubted he could hear me over the sound of Bertha.

Luckily, he saw her approaching hand just in time. He leapt upward into the midst of the cloud, causing a cascade of plastic balls to rain down, and wriggled out of sight.

A moment later Bertha's fist closed around the place

where Uncle Steven had just been. She didn't get him, but she did get the plastic bear, which she tossed into her mouth and swallowed.

"There goes our escape," said Mercy.

"MORE," cried Bertha.

I heard laughter from below us. Grandpa Gerald was perched on Bertha's broad shoulder, watching this all go down with apparent amusement.

Mercy scowled and silently waved at me to follow. We rappelled down the side of Bertha's head using her hair as ropes and landed on her shoulder beside Gerald.

His eyes flitted casually over us.

"Ah," he said. "Lovely to see you two again."

Mercy leaned close to him and sniffed.

"Now, really," he said, flinching back. "That's quite rude."

"No doubt about it," she said. "You're my real grand-father."

"I'm certainly not," Gerald protested. "Fake as the day is long."

A plastic ball bounced off my head. Bertha was grasping big handfuls of the cloud and popping them in her mouth.

"You have some explaining to do," Mercy said to Gerald, in a tone uncomfortably close to my mother yelling at me for something I did wrong. "You died. We all mourned you. My mother . . ."

She trailed off, a pained expression flitting across her face. I remembered what she'd told me, how her mother had taken Gerald's unexpected death really hard. How she'd been sleeping that grief off for years.

"You tricked us," Mercy said. She was angrier than I'd ever seen her. Not just annoyed, but really furious. "You let your own children believe you were dead. How could you be so selfish?"

You could practically hear Gerald's mind working, trying to come up with a way to weasel out of the situation.

I nudged him in the ribs with my socked foot. "Come on, dude," I said. "Be a grown-up about this. 'Fess up."

"Fine." He threw his hands in the air. "You got me. I'm sorry."

He didn't sound sorry, though.

Bertha was still furiously grasping at the sky, popping plastic balls into her mouth like sugary cereal. I thought I glimpsed a flash of light through the cloud. It twinkled for a second and then was gone.

Mercy must have seen it, too, because she pointed angrily upward. "Now the barrier's getting unstable and it's all your fault."

"Come, now," said Gerald, with a shrug. "You can't blame me. You know what the real world is like. It's so much more relaxing here."

"You can't just run away from your responsibilities like that!" Mercy shouted. I was a little worried Bertha would notice us then, but she was still distracted by the cloud. "People were depending on you. You need to go back to the real world and fix the mess you made."

"Fine," said Gerald.

"Fine?" Mercy clearly hadn't expected that response.

"Fine," he said again. "You've raised some good points. Perhaps it is time I return."

He climbed to his feet and from his pockets he pulled out several fidget spinners—a fixture of the prize counter, though the peak of their popularity was already long past. He set one spinning on his fingertip and it lifted off, hovering up into the air like a tiny helicopter.

He handed one to Mercy and one to me.

"What's this for?" I asked. An anxious feeling was growing in the pit of my stomach. The inflatable bear wasn't an option, but we still had to get back up to the cloud if we wanted to leave.

Gerald grinned. He raised his finger back up to the hovering spinner. As soon as his finger made contact, he, too, began to hover.

FEAR OF FLYING

"That should not be possible," I said. The anxious feeling was growing. I hadn't thought it possible before, but I would have welcomed any inflatable animals now.

Gerald winked down at us from where he floated, a few feet above the surface of Bertha's shoulder. "Do anything with enough conviction and it becomes possible," he said.

I didn't think that was true. At least not in the real world. But here, I suppose, confidence alone might genuinely be enough to fly.

And maybe Gerald could influence the rules of this place even more easily than we could. After all, it must have originally shaped itself entirely around him. He was the grit in the oyster, the center of everything.

"This is ridiculous," said Mercy, but she set her spinner flying and hovered up after him.

I was scared to follow them. But I also didn't want to stay here. There were no good options. No safe choice.

My head felt light. My breathing was getting too fast.

I could feel it coming like a freight train—the panic attack bearing down on me. And now I wasn't even focused on my fear of flying, I was just afraid of what I knew was coming: that terrible heart-racing feeling of uncontrollable fear.

I squeezed my eyes shut. I wanted desperately to escape, but there is no place to run to when the thing you are trying to escape is within yourself.

Fear. That was all I could think of—there was no room for anything else. My mind and body buzzed with it. The more I tried to resist it, the stronger it got.

And then I heard a voice in my head. Or rather I heard my own voice, but it was as if someone else was speaking. Maybe it was some echo of Fake Nathan. Maybe it was just the tiny rational corner of my mind that wasn't totally panicking.

Breathe, the voice seemed to say.

I AM BREATHING, I thought back. *THAT'S NOT THE PROBLEM.*

Slowly, though. Breathe in. Breathe out. Breathe in.

This is stupid, I thought. *Breathing won't solve anything.*

But all the same I found myself matching my breathing to the rhythm of the voice.

A slow breath in—my chest expanding, shoulders rising up slightly, air filling my lungs.

A slow breath out—lungs contracting, shoulders settling down.

I stopped fighting the fear. All my focus turned to breathing. My mind had room only for this one thing, this simple motion.

A strange sensation grew in my shoulders. A sort of tug—lifting when I breathed in, and then releasing when I breathed out.

I opened my eyes.

I was no longer standing on Bertha's shoulder. In fact, I wasn't standing at all. I was up in the air, at the same level as Mercy and Gerald, a few feet below the massive cloud of plastic balls.

Just visible in my peripheral vision was something even more impossible than using a fidget spinner as a means of transportation.

I had wings.

Shimmery, translucent as the fake children, they sprouted somehow from my shoulder blades and flapped steadily up and down as I breathed.

"Holy crap," I said.

I bobbled slightly in the air, holding my breath instinctively out of surprise. But as soon as I returned to normal breathing, the wings lifted me back up.

"That works, too," said Gerald, eyeing my weird new bodily accoutrement.

"We should hurry," Mercy shouted, "before Bertha spots us."

"After you," said Gerald, gesturing at the cloud with his free hand.

"No," said Mercy. "You go first."

Gerald chuckled. "Who knew my little granddaughter would grow into such a polite young lady."

"If you'd stuck around, you could have seen me grow up for yourself," Mercy snapped. "I'm not going through until you go. I don't trust you."

"Fair enough," said Gerald, with a wink. He cupped a hand around his mouth. "HEY BERTHA."

Bertha lifted her head, turning toward the voice, and spotted us.

"Get them!" Gerald shouted, and then he darted away, fast as a hummingbird. A hummingbird who is also a total jerk.

TRUST FALL

Before I could even fully comprehend what had happened, much less try to escape, Bertha snatched us both out of the sky.

Once more I tumbled into her palm, caught in a cage of closed fingers. The breath-wings disappeared from my shoulders, fear reasserting itself.

Luckily, Mercy reacted faster than me. She grabbed my arm and sprinted for Bertha's wrist, slipping through her fingers just as she opened them to pop us into her mouth. Mercy dove into Bertha's sleeve, dragging me along with her.

We clung to the fabric. Bertha emptied the contents of her hand into her mouth, but all she managed to eat was a fidget spinner.

"Well, this is less than ideal," said Mercy.

We were pressed up against Bertha's skin, protected only by the red tent of her sleeve.

"MORE," she roared.

Her arm moved, reaching up toward the cloud again.

Through the opening of Bertha's sleeve, we caught glimpses of the plastic-ball cloud. There was more light glinting through it now. The light was so bright, so real, that everything around it paled in comparison.

"It's destabilizing fast," said Mercy. "We need to get my grandfather out of here."

"How?"

"I don't know," said Mercy. She sounded as dejected as I felt. We were trapped, totally helpless, up the sleeve of a giant who seemed to have become the physical personification of Nowhere itself, all-consuming and all-powerful. We watched as Bertha ripped another handful of plastic balls from the cloud, revealing more sparks of bright light.

"Can she break through into our world?" I asked. "Because it sure looks like she wants to."

"I hope not," said Mercy. "As far as I know, fake people can only cross over if someone real pulls them through."

Which gave me an idea. Once I thought of it, I was surprised it hadn't occurred to me earlier.

"We need Bertha to help us get your grandfather," I said.

Mercy frowned at me. "Have you been paying attention? She's not going to help us. She literally ate you."

"Well, sure, but I like to think I'm mature enough to forgive."

Mercy rolled her eyes.

"She might help us, though," I said, "if we can offer her the one thing she wants the most."

"What, eating people?"

"No. What she's really hungry for is reality. Remember when we first saw her? She was eating the children's stories about our world."

"I'm not sure stories are going to be enough anymore," said Mercy.

For maybe the first time, I was one step ahead of Mercy. "Just trust me," I said. "I think I can do this." I didn't know how to explain the experience I'd just had. Mercy had seen the wings, I was pretty sure, but she couldn't know what had been going on in my head. I'd felt so helpless, so overcome by fear. But then instead of fighting the fear, I'd accepted it—I'd moved through it somehow. And that had given me power.

I felt brave. Felt like I could face my fears if I needed to.

"I guess you can try," said Mercy, though she didn't sound convinced.

I took a deep breath.

Before I could talk myself out of it, I slid to Bertha's wrist and poked my head out of her sleeve.

"Excuse me," I shouted up toward her moon of a face. "Bertha? Can we talk for a moment?"

Bertha lifted her wrist up and squinted at me with her black-hole eyes.

She was bigger than me, but so what? Jake was bigger than me and he wasn't nearly as tough as he pretended to be. He was just a confused teen who kind of hated himself and took it out on other people (or, when the opportunity arose, on his fake self).

And yes, Bertha resembled the villain of every book I'd ever read. Like so many of them, she was strange-looking, different. Not beautiful by common standards. She was also, to put it bluntly, fat. I'd been told by so many TV shows and movies, by the kids at school, by Jake, by my mother even, in a more subtle way, that being fat meant there was something wrong with me. Something I needed to grow out of. I was the "wrong" shape, and Bertha was too.

But that didn't mean she was evil.

Gerald didn't look like a villain at all. He was a charming old guy with twinkling eyes and whimsical ways. Looking at him and Bertha, most people would probably guess right away that she was the bad one, that he was the kind and helpful mentor.

But that was wrong. Gerald wasn't kind or helpful. He'd hurt people very badly and he'd done it out of pure self-interest. "No hard feelings about eating me earlier," I said to Bertha, and found, to my surprise, that I meant it. "Like, I get it. It must be really awful to be so hungry all the time."

"It is," she said. I was so close that the force of her voice caught my hair like wind. Luckily, her breath didn't smell bad, despite the enormous and peculiar variety of things she had consumed. It didn't smell like anything. "An unquenchable thirst, an unbearable ache. An emptiness more vast and hollow than you could ever comprehend."

I shivered. Bertha's endless hunger—that was Gerald's fault too. He'd created this place, let it grow, just so he wouldn't have to deal with anything difficult. "I want to make a deal," I said. "We can help you get what you really want. Because you're not actually hungry for food, right? You're hungry for reality."

She nodded.

"We can take you to the real world if you help us. You can't go through on your own, but a real person can hold your hand and pull you through."

Bertha's eyes got wide, going from backyard swimming pool size to Olympic swimming pool size.

"A real person," she echoed.

Mercy slid up beside me and jabbed me in the ribs.

"What are you doing?" she whispered. "You can't take her through."

"Why not?" I whispered back. "You take the copy of your mother into the real world."

"Yeah, but . . ." Mercy trailed off, looking conflicted. "I probably shouldn't. And Bertha is . . . I mean, I don't even know what she is, really."

Misunderstood, maybe. Only monstrous because we saw her that way.

"I don't think we can get Gerald out without her help."

"The barrier between reality and Nowhere is already so unstable," said Mercy. "What if taking her through breaks it entirely?"

"We could promise to take her through," I whispered, "but then not do it."

Mercy nodded, reluctantly. Hopefully Bertha hadn't heard me. It felt a little cruel, but it seemed like the only way.

"Your world," said Bertha. I could hear the longing in her voice. "Take me. I want to see it more than anything."

"Okay," I said to her. "We will, but we need one small favor first. All you have to do is get Gerald and shove him through the ball cloud. You know him, right?"

"Of course," she said. "In the beginning he was all there was. He told me about so many wondrous things. And that is when my hunger began."

"Exactly," I said. "It's all his fault."

"Yes," said Bertha. A look of sadness passed over her face. "I suppose it is."

She began to walk, swinging her arm back down to her side. I would have tumbled right out of the sleeve if Mercy hadn't managed to grab my leg and haul me back in. She'd pulled some of the thick woven threads of the sleeve free and tied herself in so she wouldn't fall.

We huddled just below the cuff as Bertha moved swiftly. I couldn't see much, but presently I heard a small and distant voice.

"Ah, hello," said Gerald. "Did those dreadful children leave, or did you eat them?"

There was a lurch. Bertha must have grabbed him with her other hand because his voice drew closer suddenly, though it also sounded muffled.

"Now, really!" he exclaimed. "That's hardly sporting. Are you going to eat me again, too? I have plenty of stories I could still tell you if you don't."

"No," said Bertha. "I want more."

I felt the arm we were attached to swinging upward. Unable to help myself, I slid up a little bit and peered out of the sleeve. Bertha's other fist was clenched tight, Gerald presumably inside it.

With the hand we were near, she reached up and pulled free a huge fistful of cloud. She didn't bother eating the plastic balls, but just flung them aside, nearly flinging me out of the sleeve at the same time.

Up above, the light was shining through the cloud brighter than ever. As I squinted at it, a pattern emerged. A grid of dark lines. Sort of like graph paper. Or a screen door.

Or the mesh net at the bottom of the big ball pit.

"What's going on?" Gerald shouted from within Bertha's fist. "Let me go."

But Bertha wasn't listening.

"MORE!" she cried, sounding for the first time delighted rather than furious.

I spotted a familiar face just beyond the netting in the sky, peering down.

"Oh, what the hell is going on now?" came the faint voice of Uncle Steven. "Somebody had better pay for this."

Mercy slid up beside me and squinted up at the hole in the world, at Uncle Steven staring down through it.

"Uh-oh," she said.

Jake appeared beside Uncle Steven. It was kind of like looking up at the ceiling of the Sistine Chapel, except everybody had clothes on.

"We'd better run," said Jake.

With a wordless cry, Bertha punched the fist containing Gerald straight up at the sky. There was a tearing sound and then a rush of cold air from above us, gusting down Bertha's sleeve. I hadn't fully realized before how still the air was here, how windless, and how temperate. Neither hot nor cold.

The cold wind brought with it a cacophony of odors. And yes, the word *cacophony,* which I know thanks to good old Mrs. H. is supposed to refer to a bunch of loud sounds, but it's the best I can do since the English language has no word to describe a bunch of smells. Perhaps if I spoke Dog, it would be easier.

There were more sounds now, too. The sound of Gerald screaming, yes, but also all these background noises that had been absent. I hadn't even realized they were missing until they returned. The buzzing of electric lights. The distant roar of airplanes. The gentle fizzing sound of air molecules rubbing up against each other.

Listen some time when it's really quiet if you don't believe me about that one.

There was one final sound—a loud *POP.*

And then everything vanished.

EYES ON THE INSIDE OF YOUR HEAD

When I say everything vanished, I really do mean everything.

I couldn't see Mercy. I couldn't see Bertha. I couldn't see anything, not even shades of dark or light.

I couldn't hear anything, either. Couldn't smell anything. Couldn't even feel anything. I lacked proprioception, thermoception, interoception—everything, no exception.

It was sort of like jumping into a pool full of icy water. For a moment all you know is the cold of it and you are the cold and it takes you a while to remember where your limbs are and how to use them. Except instead of water this pool was full of nothing and all I knew was the nothingness and for a while I was the nothing.

It was sort of peaceful, I guess, like Gerald had said. Mostly it was just boring. I understood how an abstract concept must feel. An abstract concept can't eat ice cream or run or play or blink or breathe or think or feel or write or read or suffer or recover or fail or succeed or slip on the ice or stub its toe or dream or dread or run its tongue along the back of its teeth or blink so fast that the whole world becomes a disco. It can't do a thing.

Thankfully, I didn't have to suffer through oblivion for long, because suddenly there was Mercy.

Well, no, that's the wrong word altogether.

Gradually there was Mercy.

First there were her eyes. That's all I could see. I don't mean that there was a pair of disembodied eyes floating in the air in front of me. Her eyes were all I could see because they were everywhere. The whole world was her eyes.

I know that sounds strange but if you've made it this far, I think you can handle a few strange things.

I focused on Mercy's eyes, all the different parts of them. The deep black of the pupil. The gray striations of the iris. Lashes. Cornea. I could see each tiny blood vessel clear enough to count the branches.

I blinked and realized that I had eyes, too, a face. I followed the line of my left shoulder down to where it became an arm and a hand. I wiggled my fingers experimentally. Like a sixteenth-century explorer sailing up to a foreign shoreline in a thick fog, I encountered the various component parts of myself as they appeared steadily from out of the nothingness. I wiggled my toes. What a joy to have toes!

"You look ridiculous," said Mercy.

She was all there now, frizzy hair and pointy elbows and khaki shirt.

"What's going on?" I asked.

She shrugged. "I think that as soon as Gerald was returned to the real world, everything that had built itself around him collapsed. This is it. As close as we can get to Nowhere in its raw state. Isn't it wonderful?"

"Um, no?"

"Look, though," she said. "It's already trying to rebuild itself."

Around us, the world slowly became.

That's it, that's the end of the sentence. Don't tell Mrs. H.

Blurry colors appeared, patterns of light and dark, vague shapes. The shapes squirmed and shifted, kaleidoscopic.

"That's us," said Mercy. "We're doing that. Just by being here." She shook her head regretfully. "Polluting the place with substance."

Some of the wiggling colors seemed almost on the point of coalescing. Would they be plastic tubes again? Another ocean of plastic balls we could jump into and escape?

Without really meaning to, I found myself thinking about *Voidjumper*. How each new level was procedurally generated—which meant it didn't exist at all until a player entered it by jumping through a void. This was kind of like that.

Mercy and I had been floating a moment before, but now we stood in a hallway. It stretched out endlessly in both directions. The walls and the floor were made of shifting colors.

This looked a lot like a *Voidjumper* level.

A door materialized on the wall to my left. I felt sure it had only appeared because I expected it to. Everything was elastic, now. New and malleable. And it was all coming from our minds.

I opened the door. Behind it was nothing.

"How do we get out?" I asked, turning back to Mercy.

She'd gotten farther away from me. I hadn't seen her move, but she was at least fifty feet down the endless hallway now.

She shrugged. "I'm in no rush."

As I watched, she seemed to recede even farther. It was the hallway moving, I realized, instead of her. It was stretching itself out, taking us apart from each other.

"Hey, come back!"

I ran down the hallway after her, though I didn't seem able to get any closer. Doors sparked into being along the walls of the hallway.

"You go ahead," called Mercy. "I think I'll stay."

"You're joking, right?"

"No," she said as she opened one of the doors. "I like it here."

She stepped through the door and was gone.

AN EVEN EMPTIER PROMISE

I threw open the door nearest to me. There didn't appear to be anything beyond it, but I steeled myself and stepped through anyway.

The world shifted around me. I was outside now. As I moved forward, pixelated trees sprouted up from the ground and grew rapidly toward the sky, which was full of shifting colors—a surreal and miraculous sunset.

"Mercy!" I shouted.

On the horizon a blocky building wavered into being— the Krazyland warehouse. I ran to it, threw open the emergency exit door, stepped through.

The world shifted again. Now I was on a beach, except the sand, when I peered closer, was made of tiny bouncy balls. There was a soda-fountain waterfall, sending a rainbow of water (or perhaps soda) frothing down into a small bay lined with mangrove-like plants made of colorful plastic tubes. Mercy was lounging in a hammock strung between two of these.

"Mercy," I said, "come on, we need to get back home."

"I don't want to," she said, pulling a pair of sunglasses from the air and putting them on.

"What about all that stuff you were saying to Gerald? About responsibility and stuff."

"He's a grown-up. I'm just a teenager. I should get to do whatever I want."

"What about your little sister?"

Mercy frowned. A hazy image of Taxi flickered at the shoreline.

"Is Taxi your sister's real name, by the way?" I asked. "I've been wondering about that."

"Oh yeah," said Mercy. "Our mother named us after the places we were born. I was born at Sisters of Mercy Hospital. My sister, well, she showed up early."

The image of Taxi waved at us, growing more distinct, taking on three dimensions.

"You need to go back for her, right?" I asked.

"She'll be fine without me." Mercy waved a dismissive hand, and the copy of Taxi simply vanished. "It's not fair that I've had to be in charge of taking care of her by myself for so long anyway."

"Well, yeah," I said, "I guess that's true. But there's a lot of good stuff in the real world."

The sea was writhing, changing, building itself up into a giant wave, which surged toward us.

I cowered, holding my hands up to protect my face. But just before the wave crashed, it disintegrated into a thousand tiny plastic balls. They rained down around us.

"You wouldn't understand," Mercy said, tumbling out of her hammock. "You're real. You're so real sometimes I start to fall asleep just looking at you."

"You're real, too."

"I know," she said from where she'd fallen into the sand. "I hate it."

And, honestly, I kind of understood. I might not be allergic to reality, but there was no doubt that sometimes it really sucked. Reality had bullies and panic attacks and birthday parties you were forced to attend against your will.

"We have to go back, though," I said, "Don't we?"

Suddenly I wasn't so sure.

The world changed again around us. It seemed unstable, ever-shifting, like it was trying to figure out what to be. We were in the halls of my elementary school. We were by the railroad tracks. We were at the Super Freeze.

"On the house," said my best friend, Rudy, handing us two chocolate cones.

I blinked at him, startled. He didn't look like the real Rudy—not that I'd ever actually seen him in person. Instead, this was a perfect replica of Rudy's *Voidjumper* avatar. His voice sounded exactly like Rudy's though.

"Stay here," he said. "Then we can hang out all the time."

I took a bite of the ice-cream cone, but it tasted like nothing. I shook my head. This wasn't really ice cream and this wasn't really Rudy.

You had to take the good with the bad, as my mother would say. Here, maybe we could avoid all the terrible things—pain and hunger and heartbreak—but we'd end up avoiding all the wonderful things, too. That's just how reality was.

"I can't stay," I said. I turned to Mercy. "And neither can you."

She took a step back, but I reached forward and grabbed her hand.

"Come on," I said. "It'll be okay. I'll help you."

"Just let me stay a little longer," she said, her voice small and pleading. "Just a little bit."

Things kept changing and writhing around us, but I didn't let go. We were ice-skating. We were on an airplane with no wings. We were walking through a museum and the paintings had the faces of everyone who had ever made fun of me at school.

"There's nothing left for you out there," they told us.

We were at the Greater Trouton Public Pool. We were

in the deep end. Inflatable piranhas flew around our heads. I was five for an instant. We were both five. We were on the merry-go-round at Plain's Amusement Park.

"Stop the ride!" I shouted.

And then we were in Mercy's kitchen, sitting at the card table. A woman stood at the stove with her back to us as several pots and pans bubbled away on the stove. Mercy stared at her with longing.

The woman knelt and pulled something from the oven, then turned to us. I saw that she was, of course, Mercy's mother.

"Stay," she said, holding out a tray of perfectly fluffy biscuits.

Mercy pulled her own hand from my grasp and reached out to take a biscuit. Her mother beamed. A family reunion. A happy ending. Everything slowed, the music swelled. Where had the music come from? It was cinematic. It was perfect.

Too perfect. This wasn't right. This wasn't real.

"NO!" I shouted and things sped back up. I grabbed Mercy by the arm again. Before, Mercy had understood the fake world far better than me, but now this world was at least halfway built from my memories, my perceptions.

For once, I knew the rules.

Pulling Mercy behind me, I lunged past the fake mother to the stove and yanked the lid off the largest pot.

Just as I expected—*because* I expected it—the pot was

full of inky blackness shot through with tiny, twinkling stars.

The void.

I didn't have a shrinking potion, but I didn't need it. The pot grew until it was enormous, until it was the whole world, with Mercy and me tiny, teetering on the edge.

"It's beautiful," she said, blinking down at the spinning stars.

"I'm sorry," I said.

"What?" she said. "Why?"

And then I pushed her.

METAMORPHOSIS

We were falling and for once I was glad. We tumbled through the void, stars streaking past until suddenly the stars weren't stars but electric lights and we were tumbling sideways along the foam-padded floor of Krazyland Kids Indoor Playplace.

I rolled to a stop and sat up. I felt heavy and uncoordinated after my extended vacation from proper gravity. Mercy sat up beside me with a groan.

We were sitting where the large ball pit used to be. All that was left of it now were torn fragments of mesh and twisted beams. Some of the nearest plastic tubes had cracked open, scattering shards of bright plastic across the floor. The whole place looked like a tornado had hit it. A very concentrated, indoor tornado.

I spotted Gerald hunched over in the corner with his hands over his face. Uncle Steven was pacing the edges of the wreckage screaming something about insurance policies into his cell phone. Jake was on his phone, too, texting furiously.

I recalled my own phone, then. It was probably gone forever. Bertha had no doubt eaten it at some point in Nowhere, and now she and everything else in that place had been swallowed by the void. Shakily, I climbed to my feet.

And that's when I saw her.

Bertha.

She was here. In the real world. When she'd punched through the sky with Gerald clutched in her fist, she must have been pulled through after him.

But she had changed. She was still large—at least six feet tall, I'd guess, and fat—but she was human size now, not a giantess. She was changed in other ways, too. Her hair was hair instead of yarn, and a more muted, natural auburn. Her eyes, which were darting around everywhere, were real eyes instead of plastic. Her dress, though still red and polka-dotted, was a well-fitting '50s-looking sort of dress instead of an endless expanse of loose fabric.

I nudged Mercy, who was still sitting dazed beside me. "Look," I said. "Should we be worried about that?"

Mercy blinked hard in the direction I pointed.

"Whoa." She staggered to her feet and nearly fell but managed to grab onto my shoulder. "Bertha!" she shouted.

Bertha smiled, as though she was genuinely delighted to see us, and picked her way carefully through the wreckage toward us.

"Hello!" she cried, in a voice that was no longer thunder, no longer superhuman. A regular human voice, melodic and brimming with joy. "Isn't this wonderful? I suppose I have you two to thank, in part, for enlightening me to my means of escape."

She held out a hand. I flinched slightly, remembering the times I'd been caught by that hand. Luckily, Bertha didn't appear offended by this.

Mercy moved forward and took her hand. Rather than shaking it however, she scrutinized it, peering close at the palm, squeezing it.

"You've got fingerprints!" she exclaimed. She dropped the hand, leaned closer to Bertha, sniffed. A look of uncomprehending wonder spread across her face. "You smell real. You *are* real. How is this possible?"

Bertha beamed. "Well, if you recall, in my wild youth I had an insatiable urge to consume all matter. This included quite a few real objects with genuine mass that had fallen through from your world. Mostly plastic balls, but also a variety of other trinkets. At the moment I broke through into your world, with the unintentional assistance of your dear grandfather, I concentrated very hard and converted all that matter into a body."

"Wow," said Mercy.

"Do you know if one of those objects was a phone?" I asked, though I suspected I already knew the answer. "With a *Voidjumper* case?"

"*Voidjumper*?" said Bertha, eyes glittering. "What is this fantastic word? You will have to teach me. Oh! Everything here is so fascinating. Look!" she pointed excitedly at something on the ground. "Dust! Isn't it the most beautiful thing you've ever seen?"

"Um . . ." I glanced at Mercy, who appeared utterly baffled. "Will you excuse us a moment?"

"Certainly," said Bertha. "My goodness, what is that?" She traipsed nimbly over toward the prize counter. Jake eyed her nervously, shuffling away.

"What do we do?" I asked Mercy.

She shook her head. "This is so weird."

I laughed. "That's an understatement."

"Well, we can't send her back," said Mercy. "She's real now. And anyway, the hole in the world has closed up—at least the one here. Can you feel it?"

I couldn't. Everything felt normal. Nothing terribly out of the ordinary. The air smelled as expected, gravity functioned as expected. But I suppose that was the point.

I glanced back at Bertha. She was holding up items from the prize counter one by one, marveling at them as though they were the greatest treasures of the world rather than plastic junk. She noticed me watching and waved excitedly, ushering me over.

I approached with caution.

"Look," she said when I got near, holding out a translucent red plastic ring. "See how the light refracts? The light here is so much brighter than it was in the other place."

"Um, Bertha," I said, "not to be, uh, rude or whatever, but do you have any intention of, you know, eating people?"

She laughed, placed a hand on her bountiful stomach. "No, no. That hunger is gone. It is such a relief. I'm dreadfully sorry, you know, about all that. Terribly embarrassing. I hope you can forgive me."

"Yeah," I said. "I mean, it happens I guess."

"Honestly," she said, "I'd happily vow never to eat another thing ever again. There is so much to see here, and to smell! I can smell things now, it is remarkable!"

Her joy at the mere fact of existing was, I had to admit, contagious. I felt guilty that I'd considered tricking her before. She had never been the villain of the story, it turned out.

"Well," I said, smiling. "You might enjoy eating ice cream, if you've never tried it."

Bertha's eyes lit up. I glanced back at Mercy, to see what she thought of all this, but she had fallen asleep in the middle of the wrecked ball pit.

It had, after all, had been quite a busy day.

AND EVERYTHING CHANGED
IN ONE WAY OR ANOTHER
AND EVERYBODY LIVED

I was glad that we'd brought Uncle Steven in on the adventure, as it saved me having to do any kind of explaining to my mother. It felt good to see her again, felt good to be home again. Good to be on solid ground.

Krazyland would need to be closed for a while for repairs, but according to Mercy, the hole in reality had completely repaired itself. The town was no longer in danger of disappearing into a massive interdimensional sinkhole. The crisis was over.

I could go back to my normal life, spending my summer the way I liked best: in the comfort and safety of my room, playing games.

But the next morning I found myself eager, surprisingly, to leave.

"Is it okay if I go visit a friend today?" I asked my mother at breakfast.

"Friend?" she said, sounding just a bit too shocked.

"Yeah," I said, "she's one of the workers at Krazyland. She's like a year or two older but she's cool."

"Wow," said Mom. "I mean, that's great. I'm glad you're making real friends for once."

"Rudy is totally a real friend," I protested. No need to mention, of course, that I had made several unreal friends as well. Unfortunately, Fake Nathan and the giant spiders had genuinely ceased to exist.

Still, meeting them had changed the way I would think about spiders from now on. And the way I'd think about myself.

"Right, uh, sorry," said Mom. "*Local* friends."

When I biked over to Mercy's house, I found the place significantly changed from the last time I'd been there.

Mercy's mother had woken up, for one thing. The shock of learning that her father was not, in fact, dead, had been enough to startle her out of her deep sleep. She was a bit groggy still, Mercy warned me, before introducing us.

Her mother sat on the couch, sipping a mug of tea. She gave me a small, sleepy half smile. She appeared a bit older and more tired than the fake version of her, but her eyes were kind.

"I'm so glad you're making friends," she said to Mercy, who rolled her eyes.

No doubt our two mothers would get along great.

We were interrupted by Bertha, who came bustling in from the kitchen. She refilled Mercy's mother's tea, then took a seat on the couch next to her and launched into an excited ramble about the breathtaking and miraculous wonder that was steam. Mercy's mother smiled and nodded along.

"Bertha's been great," Mercy told me as we slipped off into the kitchen. "Taxi loves her, and she's already offered to help out here while my mother gets back into the swing of being awake. Bertha just genuinely loves everything about being alive." Mercy shrugged. "She's kind of like the opposite of us, you know? It balances things out."

The shock of being forced back into the real world had, meanwhile, been too much for Grandpa Gerald to handle. He'd apparently spotted a mud puddle on the short walk from Krazyland to their house and immediately fainted. Bertha had carried him the rest of the way and they'd installed him in the upstairs bedroom to sleep it off.

"I want to show you something," said Mercy. She led me down to the basement and over to the wall where the broken dryer had once sat. It was gone now, leaving only a faint outline on the concrete floor.

"What happened?" I asked.

"I snuck down here last night when we first got back," Mercy explained, "to take my fake mother back through before the others saw her—she wasn't like Bertha, you know. She'd never existed long enough to develop desires of her own. And then when I was in there, I felt it again, that temptation to just stay in Nowhere and never leave.

So I grabbed this and ran out of there before I could give in." She pulled the little cat statue—the anchor—from her pocket. "And then I had Bertha put the dryer out in the alleyway for the garbagemen. This way through is sealed up for good." She tapped on the concrete to demonstrate. "I can't escape this way ever again. I know, because I tried this morning, just to see, and it didn't work."

She sounded regretful, and I could tell it had been hard for her.

"Wow," I said. "I mean, that was probably the right thing to do."

"Yeah," she said. "I don't want to end up like Gerald. Thanks, by the way, for helping . . ." She trailed off and then revised, "Well, for *forcing* me not to get stuck there back at Krazyland."

"No problem," I said. "Actually, I want to show you something, too. At my house."

"I don't know," she said. "I'm kind of tired."

"You're always tired! Come on, I swear, you'll like this."

It took a bit of convincing, but I finally talked Mercy into biking with me over to my house. And once we were there, I introduced her to my prized possession: *Voidjumper*.

"This is actually kind of cool," she said, after I'd given her a quick tutorial of the controls and booted up a fresh world for her.

"I told you."

It was an escape of sorts, to be sure, but not one with any risk of dooming the whole world to destruction. And while I enjoyed playing it by myself, it had been way more fun once I started playing with Rudy.

Mercy took to it fast. She grinned as she sent her avatar careening through the pixelated world. I went and borrowed my dad's laptop so I could log in from there and we could play together.

In the game, we ran through an endless hallway lined with doors.

"Here," I shouted. "Press *x*."

I flung open a window that had appeared between two of the doors. It looked out on a black sky, shot through with twinkling stars. The void.

Mercy ran up beside me, and on the count of three, we jumped.

ACKNOWLEDGMENTS

Shout-out to the long-defunct Go Bonkerz in State College, PA, where I first got the basic idea for this story at approximately age nine.

Many thanks to Kelsey Horton and everyone else at Delacorte Press who worked on the book.

I wrote this to bring myself some joy and silliness in a pretty dark time. For also bringing me joy and silliness in that time, I'd like to thank my Party Farm friends, Spiders the cat, Little Alex Horne, and Grian.

ABOUT THE AUTHOR

Mar Romasco-Moore is the author of *I Am the Ghost in Your House* and *Some Kind of Animal,* as well as *Ghostographs,* a collection of short stories paired with vintage photographs. *Krazyland* is her middle-grade debut. She is also an instructor at Columbus College of Art and Design.

 @MarRomasco